# The Sleepover Club

## Three fantastic Sleepover Club stories in one!

Jessica
6off

# Have you been invited to all these sleepovers?

# Mega
# Sleepover Club ③

Sleepover Girls Go Pop!
The 24-hour Sleepover Club
The Sleepover Club Sleeps Out

Lorna Read
Fiona Cummings
Narinder Dhami

*An imprint of HarperCollinsPublishers*

The Sleepover Club ® is a registered trademark of HarperCollins*Publishers* Ltd

*The Sleepover Girls go Spice* first published in Great Britain by Collins 1997
*The 24-Hour Sleepover Club* first published in Great Britain by Collins 1997
*The Sleepover Club Sleeps Out* first published in Great Britain by Collins 1997

First published in this three-in-one edition by Collins 2000

Collins is an imprint of HarperCollins*Publishers* Ltd
77-85 Fulham Palace Road, Hammersmith
London W6 8JB

The HarperCollins website address is www.harpercollins.co.uk

5 7 9 8 6 4

*The Sleepover Girls go Spice*
Text copyright © Lorna Read 1997

*The 24-Hour Sleepover Club*
Text copyright © Fiona Cummings 1997

*The Sleepover Club Sleeps Out*
Text copyright © Narinder Dhami 1997

Original series characters, plotlines and settings © Rose Impey 1997

ISBN 0 00 710904 0

The authors assert the moral right to be identified as the authors of the work.

Printed and bound in England by
Clays Ltd, St Ives plc

# Sleepover Kit List

1. Sleeping bag
2. Pillow
3. Pyjamas or a nightdress
4. Slippers
5. Toothbrush, toothpaste, soap etc
6. Towel
7. Teddy
8. A creepy story
9. Food for a midnight feast:
   chocolate, crisps, sweets, biscuits.
   In fact anything you like to eat.
10. Torch
11. Hairbrush
12. Hair things like a bobble or hairband,
    if you need them
13. Clean knickers and socks
14. Change of clothes for the next day
15. Sleepover diary and membership card

# Sleepover Girls Go Pop!

# CHAPTER ONE

Uh-oh, I can see Frankie looking at me. Well, looking's hardly the word. She's glaring like Fliss's neighbour, Mr Watson-Wade - Mr Grumpy, as we call him - does, when he thinks we've thrown crisp packets into his pond.

I know what that look means. It means I've got to tell you the truth, the whole truth and nothing but the truth, cross my heart a billion, trillion, zillion times and hope to die before Andy - that's Fliss's mum's boyfriend - discovers that his guitar is really a cardboard cut-out and my brother Stuart discovers why his saxophone won't make a sound any more!

I'm a Libran and everybody knows Librans don't like telling lies. We're the ones who believe everybody should play fair. We're always trying to keep the peace - but 'peace' is a dirty word in our house at the moment. At least, since Saturday night.

It wasn't all our fault. It was partly Dad's, for not converting the attic properly.

He's always doing weird things to our house, like moving the doors around and building extra rooms. I shouldn't be surprised to wake up one day and find out he's double-glazed me!

I'm Lyndz, by the way. That's short for Lyndsey Marianne Collins. I'm one of the five members of the Sleepover Club.

The others are Laura McKenzie, known as Kenny. She's Frankie's best friend. There's Francesca Thomas, Frankie for short, and Fliss. Fliss's full name is Felicity Sidebotham (please don't laugh, it's not fair. Anyway, she pronounces it Side-both-am).

The last person to join our gang was Rosie, alias Rosie Maria Cartwright. It was my idea that she should be allowed to join, because she was new to the area, and new to school, and didn't know anyone.

Well, we had to rescue her from the dreaded M&Ms, didn't we? Just imagine if she'd got into the clutches of our worst enemies! The Goblin - that's Emily

Berryman, one of the M&Ms - might have twitched her stupid splodgy nose and turned her into a toad or something.

Quick! I've just noticed Frankie isn't looking. Let's run out into the garden and hide in the shed, otherwise she'll want to tell you everything as usual, and I won't get a turn.

Mum calls our shed the summerhouse, now that Dad's fixed a completely gross verandah on the front, with a wonky railing. Mum's put some old chairs in and painted them streaky blue. Mediterranean blue, she calls it. It looks more like what happened in Rosie's living room when it was being painted and Jenny, her dog, wagged her tail all over the wet wall.

Right. Now listen up, as my Canadian cousin Ryan would say. He sent us a tape with his voice on at Christmas and "listen up" was his fave expression. "Hey, listen up, the snow's fifteen feet deep outside our door." Well, if the snow was that thick all round the house, the only sound you'd hear would be from up above, anyway. You'd be walking round lop-sided, with one ear raised to the ceiling, listening up for the rescue helicopters!

But it's me who needs rescuing right

now, so stop slurping that Slush-Puppy and popping that bubble-gum and I'll tell you what you really want to know.

Oh no, I've done it now! Tell me what you want, what you really, really want... That's a bit of Wannabe, by the Spice Girls. And that, unfortunately, is where the whole thing began.

Oops! I've got hiccups now and when I hic, I really, really hic. It's your fault. You shouldn't have made me laugh. What you've got to do for me now is press your thumbs very hard into the palm of my hand while I hold my breath.

There, it's worked. Not a hic in sight (or sound). As I was saying, we - the Sleepovers, that is - are crazy about the Spice Girls at the moment. In a few weeks or months, we might be crazy about somebody else, but right now, Spice is nice as far we we're concerned.

Sometimes we sneak into the studio at school when it's empty at dinnertime. We love to dance, and sometimes Dishy Dave the caretaker plays the piano for us. He's really good. He plays all these pop songs by ear. Well, with his fingers, actually. Oh no, don't make me hiccup again! We asked him if he knew any Spice Girls songs and he did. He said he really likes them, too, and he'd got their video.

He asked us what our favourite Spice song was and we had a big argument. Fliss and I love Mama. Kenny's fave is Wannabe and Rosie and Frankie think Love Thing is brilliant. Dave decided Mama was the easiest for him to play, because it's slow.

The studio's got mirrors on the walls so that dancers and gymnasts can watch themselves performing. We all struck Spice Girl poses and sang the words. Kenny can sing quite loud, though she often goes flat. Fliss and Rosie have got soft, whispery voices, but at least they're in tune.

Frankie sounds like a crow with laryngitis. No wonder she wrote in her Sleepover diary a while back that she'd given up wanting to be a pop star when she grew up and wanted to drive a taxi instead!

As for me, I think I'm a good singer. Yes, I know I sound as if I'm boasting, but I was given a solo to sing in the Nativity show last Christmas and Mrs Weaver would never have given it to me if she thought I sounded like Mary and Joseph's donkey. (Frankie does.)

Dave thought we were good. "That's great! You sound just like them," he said.

"There's five of you, too, just like the five Spice Girls. You should start a group," he said.

So, really, if we're blaming anybody, we should blame Dishy Dave for getting the ball rolling, the cookie crumbling, the group grouping ...

Okay, okay. I know I'm rambling. Please don't fall asleep, though. I haven't got a Sleepover planned for tonight. In fact, after last Friday, I don't think my parents are going to allow one here ever again!!!

# CHAPTER TWO

Right from the start, it was intended to be our thing. 'Girl Power', as the Spice Girls would say. The last thing we wanted was to get mixed up with a gang of horrible, smelly boys, even if some of them were my own brothers.

You should get a whiff of Tom's room. He's my second oldest brother, aged 14. Old socks and stale crisps. Steve, who's sixteen and my oldest brother, smells of zit cream and stinky feet, because he hates having baths.

I once made a sign for Tom's door. It had a skull and crossbones on it and under it I wrote, NASAL DEATH AREA. He took it down and ripped it up, leaving all the family noses in mortal danger once more.

Fliss and Rosie have got brothers, too, so

a few weeks ago I decided to try and find out if all brothers smell, or if it's just my personal misfortune. Fliss said that Callum, her seven-year-old brother, smells like stink bombs. My little brother Ben smells of wee, and as for baby Spike - well, he often smells of worse, when his nappy needs changing!

Rosie's got the perfect brother. Although Adam's got cerebral palsy and is in a wheelchair, he's fanatical about his appearance. He loves taking showers and having his hair moussed and gelled and the best prezzie you can give him is a really nice spray cologne. I wish my brothers would catch the habit!

It's not as if nobody ever gives Tom and Stuart any smellies. They're always getting them for Christmas and birthdays, but the minute they put them on, the scent mutates into Dead Rat or something.

Not that they often use their smellies on themselves. They do stupid things with them instead, like the time Stuart decided our cats' litter tray ponged and wasted a whole bottle of Dad's Aramis, trying to freshen it up.

Unfortunately, right in the middle of his spraying activities, Toffee came bounding through the cat flap and caught a full blast.

Fudge and Truffle, our other two cats, treated him like an alien and wouldn't go near him for days, and Buster, our dog, got a sneezing attack whenever Toffee sat next to him.

Anyway, back to that afternoon three weeks ago, which is when it all began...

The bell for the end of dinnertime had rung and we all said a reluctant goodbye to our reflections in the mirror and started to walk back to our classroom.

Fliss was the last one to leave the studio, of course. She just had to pout at herself and toss her ponytail one last time. She gave a high kick through the studio door and lost her balance and nearly fell over. As she tottered around with her arms whirling like windmills, who should stroll past but the lurv of her life, Ryan Scott.

"Hi there, Fliss. They'll never have you in the Riverdance team," he said, sniggering.

You should have seen her blush. It was just as if someone had thrown tomato ketchup in her face! Frankie gave me a big nudge and I nearly fell over, too.

"Drunk again, Lyndsey," said Ryan.

"Oh, run off and play on the M1, won't you?" said Frankie, in her best "you're being really bo-ring" voice.

He shrugged and did a big slide round the corner of the corridor, with his hands in his pockets. I was hoping Mrs Lynch would be coming round the corner and he'd go wham, straight into her, but no such luck.

Mrs Lynch is our school secretary and she's seriously bad-tempered, not like Mrs Poole, our Head. She's a sweetie, unless you do something really bad, and then she can get you expelled!

"Why did you have to be nasty to him? He'll think we don't like him now!" Fliss complained.

"I think you're a very sad person, Fliss," Frankie told her, and a row was all set to break out, until Kenny changed the subject. Thank goodness she did. Who wants to talk about boring boys? Especially big-headed posers like Ryan Scott!

What Kenny said was all set to change our lives, though none of us knew it at the time.

"Do you think Dave meant it?" she asked us.

Rosie frowned. "Meant what?"

"About us being like the Spice Girls."

"I hope so!" said Fliss.

"Stoo-pid!" said Frankie.

"Why does it matter?" I asked Kenny.

"The competition!" Kenny said.

We all stared at her. Then I suddenly remembered. I don't watch much telly. I'm not as mad about it as the rest of the club, especially Fliss, who eats, drinks and sleeps Friends and has all the episodes on video - she's the saddest thing on earth! One thing I do enjoy, though, is seeing people make complete twits of themselves on Stars in Their Eyes, where they have to look and sound like a famous singer.

The other day Mrs Poole announced in Assembly that the school was going to raise some money to send some needy kids in a children's home on holiday.

"The staff and I have had a discussion and we've come up with something we thought you'd all enjoy," she told us. "Every class is going to enter an act in Cuddington Primary's version of Stars in Their Eyes. There'll be class heats first and we want all of you to have a go. The winning act from every class will get a prize, and they'll perform in the charity show. The ticket money will go to the children's home."

We didn't think any more about it, as none of us are particularly talented, though Fliss thinks she looks and sings like Madonna and Frankie plays pretty mean piano.

But it looked as if Frankie had thought of something now, and the rest of us were desperate to find out what it was.

The door of our classroom was closing as we got to it. I grabbed the handle to stop the others from entering, while I thought quickly.

"Six o'clock at my place, folks," I told everyone. "Mum's got yoga tonight and Dad'll be in the workshop. He's trying to finish this really gross pot for Auntie Cath's birthday. I don't know what she'll ever use it for."

My dad really fancies himself as an arty potter, but his efforts are always wobbly and lopsided, or bits drop off them. They are totally useless, though he thinks they're works of art which should be worth millions of pounds and displayed in museums throughout the world.

"A spaghetti jar?" suggested practical Fliss.

"A potty?" Rosie giggled.

"That's what your dad is – a potty potter," Frankie said.

We all laughed loudly, even me, though it was my dad Frankie was insulting.

Then Mrs Weaver yelled, "When you girls feel like joining us, the class can start."

So we had to go in and pretend to be interested in caddis fly larvae.

As we were drawing them in our Nature Study books, Frankie made hers look like my baby brother Spike, swaddled in an enormous nappy. I tried so hard not to laugh when she passed it to me under the desk that I got the hiccups.

Mrs Weaver sent Alana Banana, of all people, to get me a glass of water, but my hand shook so much as I hiccuped, that the water shot all over the back of Emma Hughes, one of the M&Ms.

That put the king in the cake all right! She's one of our worst enemies and the sight of water dripping down her neck inside her collar made us have hysterics. We just collapsed with our heads on our desks and sobbed.

But it stopped my hiccups, so it was a good thing for me, if not for Emma, who hissed, "I'll get you for this, Lyndsey Collins! You've really got it coming!"

Now, a threat from the M&Ms spells real doom. I had no doubt in my mind that Emma and her crony Emily meant to do something to get back at me.

But what...?

# CHAPTER THREE

I laid the news on Mum as soon as I got home.

"No way. You can't have all your friends round tonight," she said.

"But why not?" I wailed. "I've invited them now. It's not fair!"

"I've got some of my friends coming this evening. I might be an old wrinkly, but I do have friends, you know, and I'm going to be far too busy entertaining them to cater for you lot as well," she insisted.

"I thought it was your yoga night and we wouldn't be in the way," I said.

"It's been cancelled. The teacher's on holiday."

I put on my sweetest, most pleading face. "Please, Mum... They'll have eaten already by the time they get here. And we won't take up any space. We'll go straight up to my room and disappear. We're having a summit conference," I told her importantly.

"The summit of stupidity, if you ask me!" snorted Tom, who would happen to walk into the kitchen right then.

"It is not!" I said angrily.

"'Tis."

"'Tisn't!"

"Oh, stop being babyish, you two," said Mum. "Look, if you want to see your friends tonight, Lyndsey, just make sure they bring their own crisps and biscuits, and keep out of the lounge at all costs. Okay?"

"Thanks, Mum!" I said, giving her a hug.

Frankie's dad brought her, Kenny and Rosie over. Shortly afterwards, Andy, Fliss's mum's boyfriend, dropped Fliss off.

I'd already done a phone around about the food situation, and raided some of the emergency rations Mum keeps in the spare fridge, which sits next to the huge freezer in the garage.

I'd found a big tub of my favourite ice-cream, two packets of chocolate biscuits and a bumper crisp selection pack. Don't ask me why there were crisps in the fridge. I guess Mum was being hassled by Ben and

Spike and just shoved them anywhere to get rid of them. The crisps, I mean, not my little brothers.

Frankie's dad brought in a six-pack of Cokes. Fliss had some bananas and a bottle of diet lemonade so I knew she had to be on one of her healthy eating kicks again. Rosie had some Jaffa Cakes. Kenny was carrying a weird looking cake. It was sort of pinky orange.

"Ugh! What's that?" I asked her.

"Molly made it at school. It's supposed to be carrot cake," she explained. Molly is Kenny's twelve-year-old sister.

"It's bound to be horrible," Fliss said. "She wouldn't have let you have it if it hadn't been. You know how much she hates us. She's probably trying to poison us so she'll never have to move out of the bedroom again."

Molly and Kenny share a room and every time we spend the night there, she has to move in with Emma, Kenny's oldest sister. Both of them hate having to share, and Molly's always nasty about which of her possessions we mustn't touch or go anywhere near. Last time we had a sleep-over at Kenny's, Molly was so strict about her precious Spanish costume doll that, after she'd gone, I took its knickers off and made it a little nappy out of some pieces of toilet paper held together with a safety pin.

She can't have discovered it yet, otherwise she'd have gone ballistic and I'd have heard all about it from Kenny.

I made everyone take off their shoes before going in my room. We always kick our shoes off, anyway, and my room's too small for loads of shoes. There's no space to put anything and Dad still hasn't made me the new bedroom in the attic he's been promising me for over a year.

I took the cake off Kenny and looked for somewhere to put it, where it wouldn't get damaged. My dressing table was far too full of stuff, so in the end I put the cake down on the floor, between the bottom of the bed and the window. Big mistake.

Meanwhile, everyone was cramming themselves on to my bed and on the carpet. There was no room for Rosie till we'd closed the door and she could sit with her back to it. That was great, because it meant no nosy brothers could get in.

Frankie remained standing. It was obvious she wanted to organise everything as usual.

"I've got this great idea," she announced.

We all groaned. This was one of Frankie's stock phrases, and it always led to trouble of some sort.

She ignored us. "How many Spice Girls are there?" she asked.

"Five, of course," said Rosie.

"How many of us are there?"

"Five," said Kenny, frowning.

Frankie grinned. Then she ripped open a crisp packet noisily and started cramming the contents into her mouth.

I sighed. Frankie loved 'keeping us in suspenders', as she put it.

"Come on," I said. "Give us a clue."

"Mm-mm-mm-mm," she muttered through her munching.

"What?" we asked her.

She gave a big gulp and licked her crumby lips.

"Stars in Their Eyes," she replied. "School version, of course. Why don't we go in for it as the Spice Girls?"

"Yeah! Fantastic! Can I be Baby Spice?" yelled Fliss.

She took a flying leap off the end of the bed. There was a squelchy sound. Then silence. Then an awful scream. She'd landed right in Molly's carrot cake and squashed it all over the carpet. Fliss is very fussy, just

26

like her mother. She absolutely hates getting in a mess. When we saw bits of creamy orange sponge squidging between her bare toes, we all collapsed.

"Oh no, oh no, I think I'm going to wet myself," giggled Rosie, which made us all laugh even more.

Then I heard Mum coming up the stairs.

"Girls, girls, what's going on up here? Is everything all right?" she called out.

"Yes, yes," I panted, between hoots of laughter. "Fliss just put her foot in it, that's all!"

Luckily for us, the doorbell rang. Mum dashed down the stairs to answer it, giving me a chance to get a sponge from the bathroom and do some cleaning up.

When we'd all calmed down, we got down to some serious snacking and talking.

"Who's going to be who, then?" asked Kenny.

"I think you should be Sporty Spice," Frankie told her.

Although we all like sports and all play netball, Kenny is seriously sports mad. She never wears anything but jeans and sportswear. Tonight, she was wearing jeans and a Leicester City Football Club sweatshirt. They're her favourite team. My dad and grandad are mad about them, too, and sometimes we all go to matches together.

We all agreed that Kenny was perfect for Sporty Spice and, to save arguments, we agreed that Fliss could be Baby Spice. She has the right colour of hair, after all.

It was a bit difficult choosing Ginger Spice, because none of us has got ginger hair. But my mum has a big trunk full of dressing up clothes, amongst which is a red wig she bought to wear at a fancy dress party. I felt sure she'd let me borrow it. So I became Ginger Spice.

We all thought Frankie was perfect for Scary Spice, because she's such an extrovert. Although she doesn't wear glasses, she's got some sunglasses that the lenses keep falling out of. So she said she could just wear the frames.

"Don't think I'm going to get my tongue pierced, though," she said, with a shudder.

"You could stick a blob of chewing gum on it, to look as if it was," suggested Kenny.

"Yes but when I sang, it would go flying out into the audience," Frankie said.

"It might hit one of the M&Ms," said Rosie, giggling at the thought.

"Right in the eye, with any luck," I said.

Frankie laughed and spluttered crisps everywhere. As usual, we were all getting covered in crumbs. It's as if, when we get into a room together, we become grot magnets and pick up every crumb, foodstain and drip going. It's like magic. I think every bit of dropped food and spilt drink in the universe looks around and says, "Oh look, it's the Sleepover Club, let's go get 'em!" and they all come whirling in our direction and go splot, all over us.

Four Spice Girls were decided. That left Rosie to be Posh Spice.

"But I'm not posh!" she protested.

"Your hair's the right colour, though," Fliss pointed out.

"Okay. Now, how about our clothes?" Frankie said. She was being the boss, as usual. None of us really minded, though. At least she got things done, so the rest of us could be lazy.

"Kenny's all right, she can just wear what she normally wears," said Fliss.

"And so can you, Fliss," Rosie said. "That silver dress of yours is a bit like one that Emma wears."

By 'Emma', she meant Baby Spice, of course, not Emma of the dreaded M&Ms, my very worst and dreadest enemy!

"There's always Mum's dressing-up box," I said. "Anything we haven't got, we're bound to find in there. She's even got some genuine stripy T-shirts from last time they were in fashion."

"Cool," said Frankie.

"Now that we've decided who we all are, how are we going to do our show? Mime to one of their records?" I asked.

"No way. I want to sing!" insisted Fliss.

The rest of us glared at her. We didn't want to sing and get laughed at by all the boys in our school. Of course, she hoped Ryan Scott would hear her wonderful voice and fall madly in love with her. I tell you, Fliss is saddest of the sad!

"We've got to sing. They do on Stars in Their Eyes," said Rosie. "Besides, I want to sing Say You'll Be There."

"No, we've got to do Wannabe!" yelled Frankie.

"Mama," begged Fliss.

"Okay, okay," Kenny said. "Tell you what we'll do. We'll put the CD on and try them all out and see which one we do the best."

We soon found we had a mega problem. The louder we sang, the louder we had to turn the volume up in order to hear the Spice Girls. And the more we turned it up, the louder we had to sing, until we were screeching at the tops of our voices.

I switched the machine off in the middle of Mama.

"It's no good," I said. "We'll just have to mime."

"No, no!" Fliss wailed.

"Or else get hold of a karaoke tape with just the music on," suggested Frankie.

That was the best idea anyone had had all day. In fact, we were so happy about it that we decided to eat our tub of ice cream, which was busy melting.

Before we could even pick up a spoon, doom struck in the shape of my oldest brother, Stuart. He hammered on my door and yelled, "Hey, Lyndz, you haven't seen the food that was in the fridge in the garage, have you?"

My hand shot to my mouth and I felt quite ill.

Fliss let out a squeak like an electrocuted mouse.

Frankie groaned, "Oh, no," then we all tried to be as quiet as anything.

But it was no good. Stu came barging in, totally ignoring my Keep Out notice on the door.

"Aha! Thought as much!" he said,

swooping on the ice cream. Luckily, we hadn't even got the lid off yet.

"I'll have those chocolate biscuits, please. And the big bag of crisps," he demanded.

"Er..." I went. The others had gone bright pink and were starting to giggle. "Shut up!" I hissed at them.

I saw Kenny trying to push the remains of one of the biscuit packets under the bed, but I had so much junk over there that it wouldn't go.

"Don't tell me you've scoffed the lot?" Stu said. "I've got Tony and Mick here for band practice. That food was for us. I bought it and hid it specially so that greedy pigs like you and Tom wouldn't find it."

I looked at my feet, wishing they'd disappear through a hole in the ground, with me following them. But no such luck.

"Sorry," I said. "How was I expected to know that stuff was yours? Put your name on it next time."

"Two pound fifty, that lot cost me. You can jolly well pay me back!" he said.

He went out, going, "Piglets. Oink, oink."

I could hear his foul friends laughing. Foul fiends, I should say. Who'd have brothers?

# CHAPTER FOUR

Next day, Mrs Weaver, our class teacher, said that anyone who intended to enter an act for the charity show had to tell her by the following day.

Frankie put her hand up. "Can we tell you now, Mrs Weaver?" she asked.

"Of course, Frankie," Mrs Weaver replied.

I looked round. I could see everyone was bursting with curiosity. Especially the M&Ms. Emma's eyes were just about popping out of her head and Emily's ears were flapping like Dumbo the elephant's.

"We don't want everyone to know, though. We want to keep it a secret," I said.

Mrs Weaver smiled and said, "I see. Then write down what you want to do and give it to me."

Frankie tore a page out of her general

notebook and started scribbling. She folded it up and passed it to Mrs Weaver, who unfolded it and started to read it.

My heart was racing. Please don't give the game away, PLEASE! I begged her silently, trying to use telepathic powers to get through to her.

Well, they'll never write an X-Files story about me, because my extra-sensory powers are obviously nil. The next moment, Mrs Weaver put her foot right in it by saying to Frankie, "So there's you, Felicity, Laura, Lyndsey and who's the fifth girl? I can't read your writing."

The five of us looked at each other in panic.

"It's me," Rosie squeaked.

"Rosie Cartwright," said Mrs Weaver, writing it down.

I saw the M&Ms exchange excited glances. Emma gave Emily a big smirk.

Emily - The Goblin, as we call her - nudged The Queen (that's Emily), who in turn nudged Banana, alias Alana Palmer. Then she said nastily, "I hope you don't think you're going to be the Spice Girls. We're going to be the Spice Girls. That was our idea. They pinched it, Mrs Weaver."

Kenny gave a gasp and jumped to her

feet. "We never did!" she said. "Don't tell porkies!"

I jumped up, too. "We decided days ago. We've already been practising!" I said.

Mrs Weaver waved her hand. "Now, now, girls, stop arguing," she said. "There can be more than one Spice Girls act, and may the best one win!"

Emma, my personal worst enemy since yesterday when I'd spilt water down her stupid neck, turned round. She screwed up her face and her horrid, blobby nose so that she looked like a squashed tomato, poked out her tongue at me and said, "See?"

I pulled a face back.

"So I take it you and your friends want to be the Spice Girls, too?" Mrs Weaver said.

"Yes please, Mrs Weaver," replied The Goblin, in her most sucking-up tones. Creep! She's just pathetic.

"And who else will be singing with you?" asked Mrs Weaver.

The M&Ms nudged their slave, the slimy Banana, and she put her hand up.

I looked at Rosie. She was giggling. "They've only got three Spice Girls," she said.

"I'll join you, if you like."

We all stared as Regina Hill spoke. Even

the M&Ms stared. Regina hasn't been in our class for long. Her family have only just moved to Cuddington from London and we don't know much about her, especially as she's rather quiet. So everyone was amazed when she spoke.

"Can you sing?" Emma asked her.

You could have knocked me down with a King Cone when Regina began to sing Summer Nights from Grease, all perfectly in tune. She had an awesome voice.

My eyes met Frankie's. Then I looked at Fliss, Kenny and Rosie. Everyone had the same look on their faces. Hate, pure hate.

"It's not fair!" I said at break.

"We decided to be the Spice Girls first," Frankie said crossly.

"They're just pathetic copy-cats," said Rosie, flicking her brown fringe.

"Yes, they are," Fliss added.

"Reggie-Veggie's got a good voice, though," I said.

"Reggie-Veggie! That's a good name for her," said Frankie, with a loud snort that made us all laugh. "What kind of a vegetable do you think she is?"

"A carrot," Fliss said promptly.

"Well, she is long and thin - and her hair is kind of reddish," I agreed. Before today, we'd thought she was really pretty and she'd seemed quite nice, but she'd certainly turned into a carrot now that she'd become a friend of the M&Ms.

"You know what this means, don't you?" Frankie said gloomily.

We looked at her and shook our heads. We'd never felt so depressed.

"If they're going to sing, we can't get away with only miming. We'll jolly well have to sing, too."

"Oh, no!" Kenny wailed.

"Oh good," said Fliss. "I think I sing better than Reggie-Veggie!"

We knew she wanted us to pay her compliments, but we were all fed up so nobody did.

Fliss went into a sulk and got her Banana-In-Pyjamas toy out of her bag. Her aunt in America sent it to her. Bananas In Pyjamas are very popular in America, according to Fliss's aunt. Personally, I think dressed up plastic bananas are stupid. Give me a toy pony any day. Better still, a real one.

Fliss started creating a little wedding veil for the banana, out of a piece of paper tissue. She's mad on weddings. All her toys and stuffed animals have been married at least twenty times each, to different partners. It's about time she started giving them divorces, not weddings.

I decided to cheer her up. "Of course you sing well, Fliss. We all know that."

"Perhaps we ought to give up on being the Spice Girls and think of something else," said Rosie.

"What? Give up? No way!" said Frankie. "We're not going to let ourselves be beaten by the M&Ms, are we?"

Nobody answered.

Frankie sat down on the concrete of the playground. Her bottom just missed a piece of chewing gum. She pulled a notebook and pen out of her black nylon shoulderbag. We all sat round her as she wrote two headings on the page.

The first heading said, Us. The second said, The M&Ms.

"Right," she said. "Now, think of all the reasons why our Spice Girls group is better than theirs."

"We're better than them at everything!" I said.

"We can sing," said Fliss.

"We're the greatest," said Rosie.

"They're ugly," said Kenny, and we all fell about.

"Now tell me why they're worse than us," Kenny said.

"They're ugly," said Kenny again.

When we'd stopped laughing for the second time, I said, "And pathetic."

"And copy-cats, weeds and nerds," said Fliss.

"Is this war?" asked Frankie.

"This is WAR!" we all agreed.

That night I told my mum about it. Maybe I chose a wrong moment. At the time, she was battling with a curtain that had got stuck in one of the holes inside the washing machine.

"Mm, dear. Help me with this, could you?" was all she said.

I got my head inside the machine. A corner of the material was jammed. I had a hair grip in my pocket, from my last trip to the swimming baths. I always used grips to pin my hair under my swimming cap.

I poked the grip down the hole to loosen the bunched-up material, and promptly lost it.

"Oh, that's just wonderful!" said Mum sarkily. "That's going to rattle round in there forever, now. I'll hear it every time I use the machine."

"If I use one of the fridge magnets, I might be able to get it out," I said.

I thought it was a brilliant suggestion.

Mum didn't seem to agree. "Don't you go magnetising my washing machine, Lyndsey. It's all metal in there. Every zip will stick to the drum and I won't be able to get anyone's jeans out," she said.

I had a mental image of Mum and me, each hauling on a jeans' leg, trying to pull it out of the machine. I started laughing. Then my hiccups started.

"Oh, per-lease! Not those again," said Mum.

She rolled her eyes up to the ceiling and looked so weird that I laughed and hicked even harder.

"Sor-hic-ry," I apologised.

Mum was still tugging at the curtain. Suddenly, it came free and she fell over and landed on her bottom on the floor. I roared with laughter, it was so funny.

She gave me a hurt look. "How do you know I haven't broken anything?" she said.

"You haven't got any bones in your bottom," I pointed out.

I should have remembered that Mum

knows all about anatomy, as she teaches childbirth classes.

"I might have cracked my coccyx!" she said, which made me screech so much, I nearly had an accident. But it cured my hiccups, it really did.

I wandered out to the workshop to find Dad. I told him about what the M&Ms had done to us.

"You've just got to be better than them," he said, and started to sing Tina Turner's, Simply The Best. Now, Dad really can't sing, so I put my fingers in my ears. When I took them out again he was saying a very rude word because he'd dropped his paintbrush and the pot he was painting got a big green squiggle all down it.

"Never mind. Make it look like a piece of seaweed," I suggested.

"Seaweed? It was meant to be a leaping panther," he said grumpily

If that green blob was meant to be a panther, then I'm a Brussels sprout! Still, I said nothing. I didn't want to upset his artistic temperament. Besides, I needed to ask for extra pocket money, to make up for what I'd had to give Stu!

Then I remembered a really important question I had to ask.

"Dad," I said. "Do you know where I can get a karaoke tape of the Spice Girls' songs?"

"Haven't a clue," he said. He was being a real grump-pot. I knew his runny green panther had something to do with it.

So I rang Kenny. We'd all agreed to ask our parents about karaoke tapes and report back to her.

"You were my last hope, Lyndz," she said sadly. "Have you asked Stu?"

I wouldn't have thought of asking my rotten brother if the sky was blue, because I knew I'd never get the right answer. But everything was hanging on it. "I'll report back later. Roger. Over and out," I said.

Stu's so-called 'band' was driving everyone in our house crazy. I'd seen various band members arrive and when I went up to my room, I could hear them thumping about in the attic. There was a twang and a crash, as if the guitar fell over, then a sound as if someone had dropped the drums.

And just then, like the lottery finger coming down and saying, "It's you!", I got a fantastic, ginormous, amazing idea as to how the Sleepover Club could beat everyone, especially the M&Ms, and win the school competition...

# CHAPTER FIVE

The only person I managed to get on the phone was Fliss. Everyone else was out.

"We've drawn a blank on the karaoke tapes but I've thought of something else," I told her.

"Tell me, tell me," she squeaked.

I didn't. Not straight away, anyway. Another brilliant bright idea had dawned.

"Lyndz? Are you still there?" I could hear Fliss saying.

"Yeah," I answered. Then I said, "I don't suppose by any teeny-weeny chance that you fancy the idea of a sleepover?"

"Do I? You bet! When?"

"Friday? Saturday? The sooner the better. We've got to start practising," I said.

"The class heats are in two weeks' time," she said gloomily.

Talk about dropping a bombshell! I was gobsmacked. Two weeks? We'd never have our act ready by then. Why had nobody told me?

I said those same words to Fliss.

"But Mrs Weaver mentioned it yesterday, just after all that trouble with the M&Ms," she said.

"I suppose I wasn't listening. My mind was full of hate. Kill, kill, kill! Death to the M&Ms!" I said dramatically.

"Was that what you rung me about, then? No, not about killing the M&Ms. The sleepover?" she asked me.

"No. I only just thought of that. My other great, earth-shattering idea was about the music to go with our song," I said.

"I know. You're going to ask the Spice Girls' band to play for us, I suppose," she said.

"Ho, ho. Don't be a moron," I told her. "I was listening to Stu and his friends playing the other night and - "

"You're not going to ask them?" she said. There was pure horror in her voice, as if I'd told her the M&Ms were about to be fried in toad juice and served up to her for lunch.

"Of course not! Can you imagine my big brother even setting foot in Cuddington

Primary? It would ruin his street cred for all time! But it made me think, why don't we accompany ourselves? We could borrow a guitar, and Frankie's got a keyboard..."

"But none of us can play the guitar," she pointed out.

"I know four chords. Stu showed me," I said proudly. "That's why the sleepover's got to be held here, so he can teach me some more. Will you tell Rosie and Kenny, and I'll keep trying to get Frankie. See you later, alligator!"

"In a while, crocodile," she replied.

"Have a laugh, big giraffe!" I said. It was our latest signing-off game. We kept trying to think of new animals.

"Don't get smelly pants, elephant!"

I snorted down the phone and laughed so loud, I must have deafened her. When I'd stopped laughing, which took ages, I told her I couldn't think of any more animals.

"Don't get fat, tabby cat. 'Bye!" she said, and rang off.

I stared at the receiver after she'd gone. Then I stared at the Twix bar in my other hand. How did she know I was about to eat it? It's not as if I've got a reputation for pigging out all the time... is it?

I searched the telephone for a tiny hidden

camera that could have relayed a piccy of my choc bar, but there wasn't one, of course. It was just my paranoia at being the fattest of us five friends.

Rosie's the next fattest, she's just sort of normal. Kenny is all muscle, Fliss is a natural stick insect, and Frankie is so tall that a few spare pounds wouldn't show. She's the luckiest, I think. I hope I grow taller soon.

My next big challenge was to ask Mum and Dad if I could have a sleepover. Although I kept my fingers crossed, I didn't need to because Mum was great about it.

"You know I love having the house full of girls, instead of horrid, smelly boys," she said.

I'm glad she agrees with me about boys. It must be because she's given birth to four of them - and got Dad and our dog to cope with, too!

She repeated another of her favourite sayings: "Girls are far less trouble than boys."

Though she didn't know it, she was going to regret saying that...

Next day was Saturday. We had all arranged to go to the library in the centre of

Cuddington at the same time, eleven o'clock in the morning.

I'm the furthest away, as I live in Little Wearing, whereas the others live in Cuddington itself. So I had to ask if someone would drive me over.

Dad volunteered, as he wanted to go to the art shop and buy some paints. He probably needed more green, after his accident with the leaping panther. Why paint a panther green, anyway? I suppose that's what you call 'artistic licence'.

When Dad dropped me off at the library, saying he'd pick me up in an hour, I could see two familiar bicycles fastened to the rail outside - Kenny's and Frankie's. Frankie has a new one. It's bright green, to go with her vegetarian nature. She eats so much salad that we kid her that she'll turn green one day. All over, including her hair, just like Dad's stupid panther.

We met in the music section, by the CD and tape selection.

"Look what I've found!" yelled Kenny, earning a warning frown from the man on the check-out desk.

It was a CD of football anthems. As you know, Kenny's seriously football mad. But this pointed to her being just plain mad, as

47

well.

"Ugh! You're not actually thinking of listening to that, are you?" I said. "It'll do your eardrums in."

"I find football songs inspiring," she said mysteriously.

"Oh, get her!" said Rosie.

"Haven't they got a tape on teaching yourself to sing?" I said.

Frankie was looking very pleased with herself.

"I've gone one better than that," she said.

She waved two books at me. One was called, The Piano: Learn To Play in a Week. The other was called Guitar Made Easy.

"One for you and one for me," she said.

"I don't need that," I said, pointing to the guitar book. "You know I can play some chords."

"Yes, we've heard you," said Fliss.

She was referring to a time when we'd all been round at her place and Andy, had left his guitar lying around. He only ever got it out when Fliss's mum was out, as she hated hearing him play and thought guitars made the room look untidy.

I'd picked it up and played my four chords. I thought I sounded brilliant, but when I looked round, they all had their fingers jammed in their ears and were making being sick noises. Call themselves friends? I ask you!

"Let's get the books out, anyway," said Frankie. "I certainly need to improve a bit."

"Don't forget to bring your keyboard next Friday," I reminded her. It was only small, so it was easy to carry.

"Friday's nearly a week off. Couldn't we have a practice tomorrow?" Kenny said desperately.

Our parents would only ever let us have sleepovers at weekends, so there was no chance at all of us having a proper get-together before then, if Sunday was out.

It looked as if it was, worse luck.

"I can't," Rosie said. "We're going out for the day with my gran and grandad."

"And I'm going to Alton Towers for Carl and Colin's birthday," Fliss said, then waited for our reaction.

A chorus of "You lucky thing!" came from the rest of us.

Then I thought about Carl and Colin, Fliss's twin cousins. They were a gruesome twosome, the male equivalent of the M&Ms, as they were always poking fun at Fliss and being horrid to her. Maybe she wasn't so lucky, after all!

# CHAPTER SIX

You're in school with me now. It's dinnertime. Come down the corridor with me. Ssh! Don't make any noise. Careful, your shoes are squeaking! We don't want anyone to hear.

Stop! We're right outside the door of the studio. Can you hear the the din that's going on in there? How could you miss it? It's like a load of groaning hippopotamuses - or should that be hippopotami? It's the M&Ms practising their Spice Girls routine. They're doing Wannabe and it's really pathetic.

Let's push the door open a crack and watch them dancing. They look like hippos, don't they, as well as sounding like them!

Just look at them galumphing about!

They've got old Fatty-Bum-Bum with them, which is what we call Amanda Porter. The nickname may sound a bit cruel, but you don't know Amanda. She's a horrible person, really nasty to everyone. We wouldn't care that she bought her dresses from Tents R us, if she was nice with it. But she hasn't got the niceness gene in her entire vast body. I don't know which Spice Girl she's meant to be. There isn't a Gross Spice, is there?

The only decent one among them is Regina Hill. She's not only got a good voice, she's obviously had some dancing lessons, too. Why did she have to offer to sing with them? They'd have been booed out of school if it hadn't been for her. I wish she could have sung with us. If only the Spice Girls would suddenly add a sixth girl to their group. Then we'd definitely win.

Let's tiptoe away now, before they spot us. Did you notice who's playing the piano for them? It's Dishy Dave. He's the one who started this whole thing off by saying we were good. I wonder what he thinks of the Hippo Girls? And why didn't we think of asking him to play the piano for us, instead of deciding to accompany ourselves? It just never crossed our minds, and it's too late now. The M&Ms really would accuse us of copying them then!

None of us could wait for Friday to come. We were still arguing about which song to do, but we'd more or less decided on Mama, because it was slow. That made it easier for us to sing and play. There was no way my fingers on the guitar could have kept up with the pace of Wannabe!

I was hoping - really desperately hoping - that Stuart would be going out till late, so we could use his room. That's what happened last time we had a sleepover at my place. His room is much bigger than mine, and he's got a TV and video in there, so we could have played my Spice Girls video.

When I asked him, though, he said he wasn't sure what he was doing that night.

"Meanie!" I told him.

"Who owes her big brother loads of money, eh?" he reminded me, with a yah-boo kind of expression on his spotty face. Then he held his hand up, saying, "Pay up and I might be able to afford to go out on Friday."

He knew Dad didn't give me my pocket money until Saturday, so there was no way that I could. I went to my room and had a quick sulk. Then I sorted out my sock drawer. I'd intended to do that for ages as I couldn't find any proper pairs any more and had gone to school that morning wearing one white sock and one cream one.

I'd spent all day expecting the M&Ms to notice and make fun of me, but they were far too busy boasting about how brilliant they were at being the Spice Girls, and how no other Spice Girls act stood a chance against them. They didn't know I'd seen their dancing hippos routine. They were so sad.

It got to Friday and we still didn't know if Stu was going out or not.

Tom, my next oldest brother, wasn't. He had made up his mind to enter a picture in an art competition in one of his weird magazines.

For a whole week, he'd spent every night in his room, drawing and painting. Every morning, he'd stagger down with his full waste-paper bin, dropping screwed up sheets of paper all down the stairs. I swooped on one and when I un-crumpled it,

I saw it was an amazing science fiction type of picture, complete with space ships and aliens and weird creatures with horns and antennae and tentacles, all in brilliant orange and slime green.

"Hey! Give me that back!" he shouted, and went all red with embarrassment.

"It's good," I told him. "Can I keep it?"

He looked pleased. "All right," he agreed.

I un-crumpled another one. It was seriously loony, with lots of funny purple creatures and bright red cactus plants.

"It was supposed to be Life On Mars, but it went wrong," he explained.

He snatched it out of my hand and tore it to shreds. Buster came bounding up the stairs and ate them.

"He'll be sick now. Red and purple sick, all over the carpet," Tom said, putting me right off my Coco Pops.

The first big disaster of our rehearsal was that Fliss hadn't brought the guitar.

"I looked in the shed but it wasn't there. Andy drove me here, anyway. I couldn't have brought it because he'd have seen it," she said.

At least Frankie had remembered her keyboard, so all was not lost. She reckoned it wouldn't take long to learn the tune from my tape. At least we'd still be able to practise.

Last time we'd held a sleepover at my house, we'd all been seriously into cucumber. We'd gone off it now. Celery was our new thing. It was so nice and crunchy and didn't give you the burps like cucumber did. So when Mum had asked me yesterday what kind of food we'd like, I'd told her to give us lots of celery.

Mum had made cheese and celery sandwiches, baked potatoes with pineapple and celery stuffing, and a big salad with loads of celery in.

There were two pizzas, one vegetarian, as both Frankie and I are veggie, and a ham and mushroom one for the others, plus all the usual crisps and cakes, and a huge bag of popcorn. Oh, and lots of lemonade and Coke.

"What's that?" Rosie asked, pointing to the plate in the middle of the kitchen table.

We all looked where Rosie was pointing. I'd thought it was a bit of Dad's wonky pottery which Mum had turned into a table decoration, but on close inspection, which involved prodding it a bit, it turned out to be a pile of celery sticks, arranged as a kind of mountain with the curly leaves looking like bushes on top, and tiny flakes of carrot stuck on like flowers.

"Weird!" said Frankie. "Really weird."

I had to agree with her. It was very weird indeed.

We weren't sure whether it was intended to be eaten, or just looked at, but Fudge solved it for us by leaping on the table, which she wasn't supposed to do, striding between our plates and knocking the celery heap over with her tail. After that, none of us wanted to eat it at all, as it was covered in cat hairs.

I'd told everyone to bring some Spice Girls costumes with them, so after we'd eaten the proper food, we took the crisps and things up to my room and got down to sorting out our clothes.

The bathroom's next to my bedroom. It soon got turned into an extra changing room, as it's got a big mirror in it. Fliss and Rosie were in there when suddenly we heard an ear-splitting scream!

Had they found a humongous spider in there, or was it something worse...?

# CHAPTER SEVEN

Before any of us could arm ourselves with spider-killing weapons, there was a screech of, "Get out! Go away!" and the bathroom door slammed so hard that the pictures on my bedroom wall rattled.

Well, anyone knows that spiders can't understand English. So whatever was in the bathroom had to have more intelligence than a spider. Buster? One of the cats?

When we dashed out to see what the matter was, we found my brother Tom standing there. Now, the average spider has considerably more brains than Tom. I mean, surely he could hear bumps and voices and know that the bathroom was occupied?

Of course, there isn't a lock on the door. It broke ages ago and Dad never got round to fitting a new one, though bathroom door locks are about the most important thing in a house. I mean, you don't want someone walking in when you're on the toilet, do you?

Tom was standing there like a twit, with a clean T-shirt and a pair of underpants in his hand.

"I was only going to have a bath," he complained.

"A bath? You had one last month! Don't you think it's a bit soon for another one?" I said.

"Perhaps he's got a girlfriend," Frankie said.

To my amazement, Tom went bright red.

"He has! He has! Tom's got a girlfriend, Tom's got a girlfriend," sang Frankie.

"No, I haven't!" he said.

He bolted back into his bedroom and banged his door shut, making my pictures rattle again. I plonked myself down so hard on my bed that I bounced.

"I can't believe it!" I exclaimed. "Tom? He can't have a girlfriend. He's never been interested in girls."

"He's nearly fifteen. He could be," said Kenny.

"I think he's quite hunky," said Fliss, wiggling back into my room in her silver dress and matching shoes. She thinks anything male is hunky. She probably even fancies Buster!

"Better looking than Ryan Scott?" asked Frankie.

Fliss refused to answer.

"I'm going to write Fliss Loves Tom and put it under his door," said Frankie, looking round for some paper.

"Don't you dare!" screamed Fliss, flying at her and grinding a paper plate of crisps to dust on the carpet.

"No, don't. He'll get upset. He's really shy," I told her.

I thought it was really funny, though. He'd be in for a good teasing from me tomorrow.

I tried the red wig on. Once they'd stopped laughing, the others thought I looked quite like Ginger Spice. She likes shiny clothes and I'd made a black plastic mini skirt out of a piece of bin-liner.

I wore a black T-shirt with Stu's old black leather jacket over it, and my winter boots. I was sure Stu wouldn't mind my borrowing his jacket. He hadn't worn it for ages as it had got a bit small for him. I was boiling hot, but I tried not to moan. I knew the Spice Girls wouldn't have complained. Some of their video was shot in the boiling hot desert, yet they still jumped around and danced. They're amazing. Really professional. So we had to be the same.

Frankie looked great in a leopard print T-shirt of her mother's, worn as a dress. Rosie had a black bikini top on and a black skirt which was really a stretchy jersey top of Mum's.

Kenny just had her normal clothes on, Leicester City T-shirt and track suit bottoms. She really did look like Sporty Spice.

Frankie balanced the keyboard on the windowsill. She knocked over one of my china horses, but luckily it didn't break or I'd have broken her!

I hit the power button and fast-forwarded the tape player to Mama. The second Frankie's finger hit a key, I knew we were in deepest, darkest Doom-with-a-capital-D. Instead of sounding like a keyboard, it made a buzzing sound, as if twenty thousand bluebottles were trapped in it.

"You haven't just spilt your lemonade on that, have you?" I asked her.

"No." She frowned. Then she said, "I did upset a strawberry yogurt over it yesterday..."

"You're hopeless, Frankie!" Kenny told her.

Frankie tried every note, but they all sounded the same. She had really truly wrecked it. Now what were we going to do?

"We might as well give up," said Kenny.

She cracked the tab on a can of Coke, took a swig and passed it around. We all had some. Coke often gives me the hiccups, because it's fizzy. But not this time. Even my hiccups were too depressed to hic. They stayed in my middle, in hiding.

"I want to go to the loo," said Rosie.

"Tom's in the bath," Fliss reminded her.

"I can't wait. I'm desperate!" Rosie wailed.

"There's another loo downstairs," I reminded her. "Through the kitchen and turn right."

It was the original outside loo that had been built for our old-fashioned house. You had to be tough in those days. If you wanted to go to the loo in winter, you had to grab your wellies and brolly and risk sprouting icicles between leaving the kitchen door and entering the bog.

Good old Dad had put a nice little plastic

conservatory roof over it, which meant you couldn't get wet any more. Mum hated it because horrid, slimy moss grew on it - the roof, not the loo - and she had to climb on a chair to scrub it off with a brush.

"Come with me, someone, in case I get lost," Rosie said.

"I'll come. I want to go, too," said Frankie.

Off they went, and while they were gone, Kenny, Fliss and I leafed through *Girl Power*, our Spice Girls book, to see if anything about our costumes needed changing.

By now, I'd got so hot that I'd taken Stu's leather jacket off. I slung it on the bed but it fell on the floor and guess what? It went right to the spot where the cake had got squashed. Isn't that typical? I told you what I thought about us being grot magnets! I'd just have to wipe it down before I sneaked it back on the coat hook in the hall.

"You know what?" I said to Fliss. "I reckon I could make myself a top out of the spare bits of bin-liner. I kicked them under my bed."

I knelt down to look at them. My knees got all wet from the spilt lemonade. I pulled the bits of bin-bag out. Then I remembered the scissors were in the bathroom.

And so was Tom! Now we could get our

own back on him.

I beckoned to the others and we lined up by the bathroom door, trying not to giggle.

"One, two, three," I whispered. Then I yelled, "Charge!" and we burst the door open and galloped in.

Rats! He'd gone. Only a scummy line round the bath and a steamed-up mirror told us he'd ever been in there at all.

I got the scissors, laid the bin-liner on the floor and started to cut.

"That's funny," I said. "It's only plastic. It should be easier to cut than this."

Kenny had gone a funny shade. Sort of pale, with her eyes all bulgy as if she'd seen something nasty. "Er, Lyndz..." she said.

"What?" I frowned at her, wondering why she was looking at me like that. Had someone - The Goblin, perhaps - just turned me into a toad without me knowing anything about it?

I snatched up the piece of black plastic I'd been cutting. I realised what had gone wrong when my stripy cotton rug came up with it. I'd managed to cut through that as well.

"Mum's going to murder me!" I said, my face going as pale with horror as Kenny's.

"If you put some things on it, maybe she

won't notice," Fliss said.

There normally were loads of things on my carpet, like books and shoes. Fliss was right. I started to breathe normally again.

There was a knock on my door. "Reggie-Veggie!" said Frankie's voice. It was our password for the night. We always had one, for every sleepover, to keep out people we didn't want to come in.

"Enter, Friend!" I said.

Frankie and Rosie were looking really pleased with themselves.

"I think I've solved all our problems!" Frankie said.

# CHAPTER EIGHT

I don't know about you, but when someone says they've solved all my problems, I expect them to have come up with something really good. Instead, Frankie and Rosie stood in the doorway arguing.

"It was me who heard it first!" Rosie said, looking indignantly at Frankie.

"Heard what?" I asked, shooting Fliss and Kenny a look which said quite plainly that these two had left their brains behind in the outside bog.

"We were passing the door of the babies' room when we heard it," Rosie went on.

She meant the room where my two little brothers, four-year-old Ben and baby Spike, sleep. It's on a kind of half landing, between the ground floor and the floor where my bedroom is.

"It was in tune with the album. We could still hear the song as we went downstairs. Couldn't we, Rosie?" Frankie said.

"I haven't a clue what you mean," I said.

"A musical instrument. As in bong-plink," said Frankie, giving me a pitying look.

Bong-plink? I couldn't think of anything that went bong-plink, unless it was her keyboard being thrown out of the window.

We all went down to listen, but we couldn't hear a thing. The babies slept with their door ajar. I went in. Ben had fallen asleep with his xylophone on the bed next to him and the stick to bong it with still in his hand.

I gently slipped it out of his fingers while Frankie picked up the xylophone. We all tiptoed away.

Back in my room, Frankie hit a few bongs and plinks and began to sing - or rather, groan - Mama.

"We can't use this!" I cried. "It's a baby's instrument. Everyone would laugh. The M&Ms would wet themselves!"

Everyone except Frankie agreed with me. She continued to play it. We all joined in singing. Suddenly, I saw the funny side and started laughing. That set everyone else off, until we were rolling about on the bed and on the floor, kicking our legs in the air and shrieking helplessly.

Next moment, there was a thunderous knocking on my door. We all held our breath, trying to stop laughing. It was Mum. She came in, looking very cross. Some extremely loud wailing was coming from somewhere behind her.

"What's this about you taking Ben's xylophone off him?" she said. "He came downstairs to find me, crying his eyes out."

Her eyes swept the room, till they reached Frankie, who was trying to hide it under a cushion.

Mum swooped on it. "Here you are, darling," she said.

My little brother appeared in the doorway and snatched the instrument to his chest. His big, wet eyes looked accusingly at me.

"But he was asleep when I took it!" I said.

"Wasn't asleep!" said Ben.

"Come back to bed, darling," Mum said, taking his hot, sticky hand. "And as for you, it's time you got those clothes off and started thinking about bed yourselves. You're making far too much noise. Spike's awake now, as well."

"But it's much too early to go to bed," I grumbled.

Trust Rosie to give a great big yawn!

"See? Someone's tired," Mum said. "Now, I want to see this bedroom light off, next time I come upstairs."

"Yes, Mum," I said.

It wasn't like my easy-going mother to get cross, but I'd heard her having a row with Dad earlier. She'd asked him the fatal question, when was our house ever going to get finished? She said she was sick of tripping over ladders and paintpots and never knowing where a door or window was going to appear next. I didn't hear any answer, I guess Dad had just shrugged and looked vague as usual.

We felt quite depressed, what with the ticking-off from Mum, and not being able to rehearse. So we all got washed and into our jim-jams, and then into our sleeping bags.

Usually, when there's a sleepover at my place my bed is taken right out and we all line up on the carpet. But tonight Dad had forgotten.

I decided there was enough room for two in my bed, one at either end. We did a dip-dip-dip to decide who it should be.

Just my luck to be landed with Lanky

Frankie, the tallest of us all. It was her big, smelly feet I was going to have to put up with next to my face all night.

Before we even tried to get off to sleep, we sang our club song, which we had to do all the hand movements to.

"Down by the river there's a hanky-pankyyy,
With a bull-frog sitting near the hanky-pankyyy.
With an ooh-ah, ooh-ah, hey, Mrs Zippy, with a 1-2-3 OUT!"

We sing the song sitting up, and on the word OUT! we all lie down as fast as we can. The first one to lie down turns off her torch, then everyone else turns theirs off until everyone's torch is out.

Then we start the serious business of trying to go to sleep, which involves Rosie twizzling around this way and that, until she finally curls up in a ball with her thumb in her mouth, while Kenny makes noises like a dog with a cold, snuffling and grumping.

Luckily for me, Frankie falls asleep in one position and stays that way all night. Sometimes Fliss has a nightmare. She'll sit bolt upright and scream, terrifying the rest of us.

Tonight, though, nobody made a sound. It was as if they were all dead. Then, through the darkness, came a whisper.

"Is anybody asleep?"

There was a chorus of whispers back. "No," we all said.

I flicked on the bedside lamp. Then I heard Mum coming back up the stairs, so I switched it off again and we all lay dead still, except that the bed was shaking as Frankie was trying not to giggle.

We heard Mum flush the loo. Then she went back downstairs. I switched the lamp on again and we all sighed with relief.

"Anyone got any food left?" Kenny asked. "I'm starving."

"So are we," said Fliss and Rosie.

"And me," Frankie joined in.

I found some cheese and onion crisps and half a carton of orange juice, so we shared them out.

Then we tried to go to sleep again, but none of us could. Rosie started humming Mama and one by one, the others joined in. Oh, why did the M&Ms have Dave playing piano for them? I thought. It just wasn't fair! Here were we with no piano, not even

Frankie's keyboard. Not even a guitar.

Suddenly, I thought about Stuart's group. All the instruments were lying about upstairs in the attic, just begging to be played. Stu was out - yes, my rotten brother had gone out after all, and hadn't told me, so I could use his room.

Mum and Dad were down on the ground floor. They'd never hear. Tom would think it was Stu, come back with his friends, and he wouldn't dare interrupt them.

It was a shiny-bright, mega-brilliant opportunity. All I had to do was find the chords to Mama on the guitar and we'd be sure to win our class heat and be allowed to sing in the charity show.

My pillow felt lumpy. I felt beneath it and guess what? There was a big bag of squashed marshmallows stuffed under it. Someone must have hidden them earlier, intending to scoff them in secret later on. It wasn't me.

Did I hear you say, "For a change"? You did? That's really mean of you. I don't pig out all the time. Just most of it. I don't eat when I'm asleep.

"Hey, everyone," I said. "I've found some marshmallows." See? I'm a generous, caring, sharing person!

I switched my bedside light on again.
Everyone was already sitting up, waiting
for a marshmallow.

"In a minute," I said. "First of all we've got
a quest."

We all love stories with quests in, where
the knight has to ride round the kingdom
until he's slayed the dragon, or saved the
princess.

"Ooh!" said Rosie. "What is it?"

"To get up to the attic and shut ourselves
in, without being heard. And then we're
really going to rehearse!"

# CHAPTER NINE

It wasn't easy getting five people up to the attic in total silence. There isn't even a real staircase, just a kind of ladder that Dad made, while he's thinking of where to position the proper stairs. We might get stairs in ten years' time, just as I might get my new attic bedroom by the time I've grown up and left home!

The floor of our loft is covered in hardboard and a motheaten old carpet covers a lot of it. At least it's got electric light. If we'd had to use torches, it would have been dead spooky.

I pressed the switch and a bare lightbulb lit up. It dangled from a cord draped over one of the rafters. There wasn't any furniture up there, apart from two old plastic chairs which used to live in the garden.

There were probably loads of spiders lurking in corners. It didn't pay to look too closely.

I carefully closed the hatchway.

"Look at that!" I said.

"Wow!" exclaimed Rosie.

All the instruments a band could ever need were lying there where Stu and his mates had left them. Stu's saxophone was on the floor, propped against the bass drum. The guitar was leaning against the side of the water tank.

There was a bass guitar, too, which Frankie picked up.

"This is easy, it's only got four strings," she said, and twanged them. "How do you plug it in?" she asked.

I didn't know. But what I did know was how to plug in the tape player which Stu had left up there. It was a far more complicated one than mine and it had two cassettes in it.

I took one out. It had no label on it saying what it was, so I chucked it on the floor and put the Spice Girls tape on. The music sounded great, up in the echoey attic.

"There aren't any bats up here, are there?" asked Fliss, glancing nervously at the rafters.

"We found a dead pigeon when we first moved in," I told her, and watched her shudder.

"How about ghosts?" asked Fliss. She's genuinely scared of them, and can't watch spooky films, not even Gremlins, or Ghostbusters.

Just then the wind blew and rustled some polythene Dad had used to cover a hole he'd cut in the roof. Fliss screamed. The rest of us laughed at her.

"I'm cold," Rosie complained.

"You won't be in a minute," I said.

It was draughty in the attic, and we were only wearing our pyjamas. But I switched the Spice Girls on and as soon as we started to dance, we warmed up.

Frankie picked up the bass guitar and danced around with it. She made great swoops of her hand and bashed the strings. She looked like a real rock star.

Kenny got behind the drums. There was a slight crunch as she accidentally trod on the tape I'd taken out of Stu's cassette machine.

"Oh dear," she said.

"Don't worry, it's a blank one," I told her. Kenny looked perfect as a drummer.

"Go, girl, go!" Fliss shouted, as she picked up some drumsticks and took a wild swipe at the cymbal.

She hit it so hard that it fell off its stand. Fliss laughed so much that she had to get down and roll on the floor. When she stood up again, she was covered in dust and started coughing like mad.

"Bash her on the back," Kenny said to me, as I was nearest.

So I hit her.

"Ow! That really hurt, Lyndz," she complained.

"Sorry, I was only trying to help," I said. Honestly, you go off people sometimes! Especially when they're coughing in your face and their breath smells of cheese and onion crisps.

"Hey, Lyndz! The music's stopped!" yelled Frankie. "Shall I turn the tape over?"

"No! Don't touch a thing. Let me do it," I said.

I couldn't risk letting anyone break Stu's tape player. I was already deep in deadly debt to him, to the tune of a couple of quid. Imagine if I owed him hundreds of pounds! I'd still be paying him back by the time I left school!

I turned the tape over and pressed the Start button. Soon, the words of Mama were floating out and we all joined in.

"Turn it up louder," begged Rosie.

I turned it up a bit more. Not too much. I didn't want my parents to know we were up here. We'd have got into real trouble.

But, now that the music was louder, we really got into it. We'd never sung so well in our lives.

"Mama I love you, Mama my friend..."

We sounded better than the Spice Girls. Much better. But then, they didn't have an echoey, spidery attic to sing in, only a recording studio.

"Let's put it on again," said Fliss, when the track came to an end.

"Okay," I said, even though Who Do You Think You Are had started, which was good to dance to and always made me think of Ryan Scott. ("Who do you think you are? Some kind of superstar?" That was Ryan Scott to a T!)

I'd spotted a guitar propped up in the corner. It wasn't an electric one, so I knew I could play it. As soon as the record started, I fumbled around, trying to find the chords. The guitar wasn't quite in tune with the song.

"Stop a minute!" I shouted.

Everybody groaned.

"I was just getting into that," Frankie complained.

"Hard luck. I've got to tune this guitar," I said.

Luckily, I knew how to do it because I'd watched Stu's friend. I twiddled the knobs and the pitch of the strings went up or down. Soon, it sounded reasonably okay.

I put Mama back on again and began experimenting with the four chords I knew. And, miracle of miracles, with a bit more fumbling, I could just about play it!

"I've got it!" I said. "We can do our Spice Girls act after all! Just so long as I can borrow this guitar."

If Stu's mate had said "No," I'd have taken it anyway. Anything to beat the pathetic M&Ms.

"We'd better run through the song one more time, without the record," Kenny said sensibly.

"Yes. I couldn't hear my singing above your horrible croak," Fliss said to Kenny.

Kenny poked her tongue out at Fliss. It looked as though a scrap might break out, so I quickly picked up the guitar.

This was the real test. And, do you know what? We sounded great. When Frankie started sounding like a sick crow, Kenny nudged her hard in the middle to shut her up a bit. Rosie, Fliss and myself were in tune, and Kenny was most of the time.

When we'd got to the end of the song, I put the guitar down on the floor and jumped up in the air.

"Oh, wow!" I said.

"Yeah, wow!" said Kenny.

"Brilliant!" said Rosie.

We all hugged each other and started hopping round in a circle. Big mistake. For that's when it happened. Kenny gave an blood-curdling screech - and started to disappear before our eyes!

# CHAPTER TEN

"Kenny!" I shrieked, grabbing at her.

The others were all rushing round flapping like headless chickens.

"Frankie! Help me!" I yelled, as I hung on to Kenny for dear life.

Now that I was next to her, I could see what had happened. It was all Dad's fault, as usual. There was just one place in the whole attic where he hadn't put any hardboard, and Kenny's foot had found it and gone between the rafters and through the flimsy floor.

"She's not going to fall down to the next floor, is she?" Rosie asked anxiously.

"Don't move!" I ordered Kenny.

"Just as if I could! Isn't anyone going to

ask if I'm all right?" Kenny said. Although she's the toughest one of us, her voice sounded quite wobbly.

"Er... are you all right?" I asked her. I was still clutching her arm, trying to save her.

"I would be if you'd just let go. Your fingers are digging into me," she said.

"All right, all right. I was just trying to stop you falling forty thousand feet into the Pit of Hell!" I said.

I let go. She didn't seem to be falling any further.

"Can you get up, Kenny?" Fliss asked.

She was in a funny position with one leg spread out at an angle. She tried to heave herself up, but it was no good.

"My leg's completely stuck in the hole," she said. "It doesn't hurt, it's just stuck and I can't move it."

"Let's have a go at pulling her out," Frankie suggested.

"Yes, we'll treat it as a tug-o'war," said Fliss.

"Don't you dare! What do you think I am? A piece of rope?" said Kenny.

I took hold of one of her arms and Rosie grabbed the other. Frankie got her leg. Fliss stood there and counted.

"One... two... three... PULL!"

"OUCH!" screeched Kenny as we all heaved as hard as we could.

But Kenny didn't budge and we all lost our grip on her and fell over.

Frankie fell on top of Kenny, adding major squashing to her list of injuries.

Rosie grabbed hold of something to save herself. It was an amplifier which we'd used as a table for the food. The marshmallows fell right into the mouth of the saxophone, followed by Rosie's wildly waving arm. Her hand went right down inside it, wedging the marshmallows in there for ever.

As she tried to get up, she kicked the drumkit. Bits flew off and clattered all over the floor.

I cannoned into Fliss. She staggered backwards and - oh, no! There was a terrifying crunching sound.

"Wh-what have you done?" I asked her, my voice all shaky with terror. I knew from the noise that something had got broken. Something that spelled major T-R-O-U-B-L-E.

I was right.

"I've trodden on the guitar. Look at it!" Rosie said. She went pale and started to cry.

I felt like being sick. She'd trodden on the neck of the instrument and it had broken in two. It was absolutely ruined. How were we ever going to pay for a new one?

Rosie was down on her knees, examining the damage.

"How are we going to do our Spice Girls routine now? The M&Ms will win and nobody will hear me sing!" Fliss wailed.

I thought personally that the school might be very glad not to hear Fliss sing - but none of us wanted the gruesome M&Ms to triumph over us. Beaten by our worst enemies! It was a fate worse than death.

"Maybe I can borrow Andy's guitar," I said to Fliss, who'd joined Rosie on the floor to inspect the broken guitar.

"This is Andy's guitar," she said doomily. "Look..."

She pointed to a label inside it. Andy's name and telephone number were on it.

"He must have done that in case he lost it," she said.

I got cross then. "Fancy lending it to Stu's group. What a daft thing to do. He might have known something would happen to it," I said.

"Stop worrying about a stupid guitar. What about me?" said a lonely voice from the corner of the attic.

Poor old Kenny. We'd forgotten all about her!

"Maybe, if we make the hole a bit bigger, we could get her leg out," Frankie suggested.

"Okay, let's have a go," I said.

Just as we were about to start our Kenny Rescue Mission, we heard the one sound we didn't want to hear.

Voices on the landing below us. Boys' voices.

"Ssh!" I hissed warningly.

We all fell dead silent.

Then: "Hey! There's a leg sticking through my ceiling!"

The yell came from Tom's room. He must have just gone in there.

Pandemonium broke out on the floor below as Stu and his mates all rushed in to see. The next minute, they were all pounding up the stairs into the attic. Our doom was sealed.

"Quick!" I said to the others. "Try and get the drumkit back together. And hide the guitar!"

"I don't want boys to see me in my pyjamas!" wailed Fliss, hiding behind the amplifier. None of us did. It was seriously embarrassing. But there wasn't a thing any of us could do about it.

The hatchway door flew open with a bang and my oldest brother stuck his head through.

"I might have known!" he shouted. "Trust you and your friends to cause trouble, Lyndz. I hope making a hole in the ceiling is all you've done..."

We all looked at one another guiltily. The wrecked guitar was behind Rosie. She'd better not budge one inch, or all would be revealed! We had to get away from the scene of crime as quickly as possible.

"Stu, it wasn't Kenny's fault that she fell through the ceiling. Dad hadn't put any hardboard there," I said.

"Well, I knew that bit wasn't safe. Why didn't you look where you were going? I suppose we'd better get her out. Mick, Tony, give us a hand, will you?"

The boys broke off a few bits of floor and ceiling and soon had Kenny free.

There was another yell from Tom downstairs. "Hey! All those bits of ceiling went all over my best painting. It's ruined! The paint was still wet," he moaned. "How can I go in for the competition now?"

I felt doom strike again. I knew I'd never hear the end of it now. Tom would never forgive me.

At least Kenny was okay, though. Now we just had the broken guitar to deal with. Or so we thought...

"Before I go and tell Mum and Dad about all this, what were you doing up here in the first place?" Stu asked me.

"We were rehearsing for a charity show at school. All the best acts get entered in it. We're going to be the Spice Girls," I told him.

"Well, the Spice Girls had better get to bed because it's nearly ten o'clock and we're going to have an hour's band practice ourselves," Stu said.

Oh no! The drumkit would fall apart the moment Mick touched it. And what about Andy's guitar?

"What are you waiting for? We want to get started. Get going, you lot!" Stu said.

Rosie didn't dare move. Her face was panic-stricken. Her lips formed the words, "What am I going to do?"

Some delaying tactics were needed.

"Just let me get my Spice Girls tape," I said, moving towards the tape player.

My brother looked as if he'd just heard that the universe was going to end in five minutes' time. He went white.

"You haven't been playing your Spice Girls tape on that machine over there, have you?" he said faintly.

"Uh-huh," I said.

There was a moment's total silence. Then his face grew fiery red.

"You idiot! You twit! You total amoeba-brain. How could you? Do you know what you've done?" he thundered.

I shook my head.

"That's a very complex machine which we borrowed from another band. We had it specially set up to record our music on. You've wiped out our demo tape that we were going to send to a record company. It took us three weeks to record. I'll get you for this, Lyndz!"

He took a step towards me, meaning to pull my hair or something. I ducked, he staggered and - guess what? - his enormous great foot stamped right on to Andy's guitar. Ker-unch!

Whoopee! A huge weight lifted off me. Now it was Stuart's turn to look scared and guilty.

"Oh crikey," he said. "Look what I've gone and done."

"I told you to put it back in its case," Tony said. "But you said you couldn't find it."

Just then, Mum and Dad arrived on the scene and we were all in trouble - all except for Tom. Everyone was very sympathetic about his painting and Dad helped him clear all the rubble out of his bedroom.

Mum ticked us off good and proper. "You girls had no right to go up there. You should be asleep in bed!" she said.

Then she started fussing over Kenny, who had a few nasty bruises. Out came the Savlon and then she offered us a real treat - hot chocolate. Not just for Kenny, but for all of us, because we were all shivering with cold by now. Yum!

But, just as she was bringing in the tray, her toe caught in something and she tripped. Five mugs of steaming hot chocolate leapt off the tray like horses tackling a six foot fence. Up into the air they went, spraying chocolate all over my bedroom wall.

Our mouths fell open in horror, and stayed that way as the mugs descended in slow motion on to my white bedspread. A brown, sludgy oasis of chocolate formed a widening pool. I stared at it, horrified.

"Don't just stand there gawping like goldfish. Help me clear up, girls!" snapped Mum.

No mugs were broken. Mum thought it was her fault, and kept apologising as she took the wet bedding away and brought in the spare duvet.

It was the last of the hot chocolate, worse luck. She'd emptied the tin. Still apologising, Mum saw that we were all tucked up in our respective sleeping places.

She was just standing with her hand on the light switch, about to say goodnight and turn it out, when it suddenly occurred to her to ask a question: "I wonder what I caught my foot on? Whatever it is, it's dangerous and I'd better find it before there are any more accidents."

Well, I lay there feeling completely innocent. So much else had happened that evening that I had forgotten all about chopping up my rug with the scissors.

Mum found it, of course. And then came the real punishment. There were to be no more sleepovers in our house, ever again. Mind you, that's what she said last time, so I didn't really believe her. But you never know with Mums...

She confiscated my Spice Girls tape, too. And my video of them. That meant we didn't have the words to Mama, because they were written down on the inner sleeve of the cassette. So it was bye-bye competition, especially as we had no chance of borrowing a guitar from anyone.

I could just see the M&Ms and their witchy friends, smirking all over their fat faces when they discovered we'd dropped out and they were the only Spice Girls after all. Emma had got her revenge. Hate, hate, hate!

# THE END

So that's it! We're all grounded again.

Stu says I owe him all my pocket money for ever and ever, for those crisps and things we ate the other day, and for ruining his band's demo tape. It's really unfair! How were we to know that we'd recorded the Spice Girls over one copy and that Kenny had trodden on the other? Fancy him not bothering to put a label on something as important as a demo tape.

Tom was beastly to me about his ruined painting, until I told him I thought the orange and slime green one he'd let me keep was even better. In the end he agreed with me, ironed out the creases and sent it off to the competition. I hope he wins, I really do.

In the meantime, Stu's given him his first real 'commission', which is when someone asks an artist to paint them something. He's asked Tom to paint a Spanish guitar. On cardboard, so it'll be stiff. It's going inside Andy's guitar case while his real guitar is being mended. It's just in case he comes round and asks if his guitar's okay. Stu will open the case and flash the piccy at him, then close it again quick!

Talking of Stu, he couldn't get a note out of his saxophone yesterday, so he's taken it into a repair shop - where, of course, they'll find loads of squishy marshmallows jammed down inside it. Uh-oh, more trouble!

Just in case you're thinking things are all doom and gloom, though, get this! Remember I told you we'd accidentally recorded the Spice Girls over Stu's demo tape? I managed to sneak up to the attic and grab it, which meant we could still rehearse. As we're currently banned from visiting each other, we stayed on late at school and persuaded Dishy Dave to play Mama for us on the piano, promising him a mega bar of his favourite choc.

A nasty throat bug has been sweeping school. We were praying that none of us would get it before the class heats. Luckily, we didn't. The heats were held in the school hall. Dave played the piano for us and I think we did Mama brilliantly. We'd changed into our Spice outfits, and the M&Ms hadn't thought of that. They were still in their ordinary school clothes.

When it came to the M&Ms' turn to perform Wannabe, we all looked at each other, scarcely breathing. This was it! We just had to be better than them, we had to! But they had Regina, whose voice is so much better than any of ours.

Dave played the introductory bars, Regina opened her mouth to sing - and no sound came out. Not a squeak. She'd caught the dreaded throat bug! Talk about laugh. We nearly had awful accidents, we laughed so hard. Luckily, we weren't the only ones laughing, or Mrs Weaver would have told us off.

They couldn't perform, so they were out of the contest. You should have seen their faces - especially when we ended up winning the class heat!

Now we go forward to the Grand Final in three weeks' time. Wish us luck! We've all decided it doesn't matter if we don't win, because we've done what we really wanted to do already. We've beaten the M&Ms and that's the best thing of all and something we'll gloat over for centuries.

Uh-oh, we'll have to scatter. I can hear Frankie charging down the path like a rhino in Doc Martens.

"Lyndz, Lyndz, where are you?" she's yelling. "You haven't seen my Nature exercise book, have you?"

I borrowed it so that I could copy her picture of a chaffinch. It was a very good drawing. She'd coloured it in with pastels. But pastels rub off, don't they? And I've just found out I've been sitting on the notebook all the time I've been talking to you. Look! There's no chaffinch left, just a nasty brown and pink smear. See that big bush over there? If I'm not around for dinner tonight, it means I'm still hiding behind it.

END

# The 24-Hour
# Sleepover Club

# CHAPTER ONE

I hope I haven't kept you waiting. It's a miracle that I'm here at all. With the strop that my parents are in, I never thought I'd see daylight again! Well, I suppose we did go a bit far this time. Quick! Keep your head down and we'll just hurry past the park gates. Phew! Right let's sit down and catch our breath and I'll tell you all about it.

Thanks to our 24-hour sleepover, I'm banned from that park. We *all* are. All the members of the Sleepover Club that is. The Fearless Five my dad calls us, or at least he used to. Now it's the Flipping Stupid Five! OK, what we did was a bit OTT. But we were only trying to get even with our deadly rivals Emma Hughes and Emily Berryman, or as we call them, the M&Ms. How were we to know that flinging a few jellies and spraying a bit of *Silly String* would cause so much chaos? Still, it was worth it to see the look on their faces. Wicked!

It all started with us planning our 24-hour sleepover. That is probably the most important date on our calendar because it's kind of where the whole Sleepover Club began.

You remember Kenny, don't you? You know, the crazy one. Well, we've been best friends for ever. When we were both about five or six and the funfair came to Abbey Park in Leicester, I went to it with her family. Then I stayed the night at her house. I hadn't really slept away from home before and I thought it was pretty cool. The next year we went to the fair with my parents and Kenny stayed at my house. Well, then we started hanging around with Lyndz at school. She's such a scream, although she's kind with it. And Fliss kind of tagged along. You couldn't possibly forget Fliss, she's so tidy and organised. She's probably the only person in the world who matches the colour of her knickers to the rest of her clothes!

The first sleepover we all had together was after we'd been to the funfair. It was class! That's when we decided we ought to form the Sleepover Club. We have heaps of sleepovers now, but this one is our anniversary. That's why we have a 24-hour sleepover, to make it special. We go to the funfair in Leicester on Saturday night, then on Sunday we have a picnic by ourselves in the local park.

This will be Rosie's first 24-hour sleepover. Of course you remember Rosie. She's new and she seemed like a bit of a wet weekend at first. She's actually pretty smart. And sensible too, which makes a change from the others!

"Francesca, you're straying from the point!" my teacher, Mrs Weaver, would say. People only ever call me Francesca when they're cross with me. You can call me Frankie.

Anyway, you want to know why we're banned from the park, don't you? And the funfair as well, actually. You might as well make yourself comfortable because we'll be here for a while.

We always know roughly when we're going to have our 24-hour sleepover because the fair comes around the same week every year. But as soon as we find out the exact dates we get a bit wild. The thing is, we're a bit hyper anyway because it's towards the end of the summer term and we know we've got the summer holidays to look forward to. Bliss!

This year, Kenny rushed up to us in the playground before school all red in the face and grinning from ear to ear. She shoved a crumpled poster of the fair at me. She said it *just happened* to have fallen off a fence as she walked past.

"The sleepover's on for Saturday the 6th," she shrieked, jumping up and down on the spot. Lyndz, Fliss and me screamed and did high fives.

"I don't see what's so special," said Rosie, looking at the rest of us as though we'd just escaped from a zoo. "We're always having sleepovers."

"Yeah, but this one isn't just a case of come in, stay the night, go home again," said Kenny. "We've got *a whole day* together doing exactly what *we* want to do."

"Oh right, so you get to be a doctor and Fliss gets married to Ryan Scott, does she?" asked Rosie innocently.

"But I'm not old enough to get married," said Fliss.

"Derr!" said the rest of us together, tapping our heads. Fliss, as you probably remember, had her sense of humour removed at birth.

"No, it's just cool hanging out together. Like *Friends*," I said.

"With no boys," added Lyndz. She has four

brothers and, as far as she is concerned, boys are a serious waste of space.

"Just Molly The Monster instead," said Fliss.

We all groaned. Molly is Kenny's sister from hell. She's only a year or so older than Kenny but they're about as different as Oasis and the BBC Symphony Orchestra. The worst thing is that they share a bedroom so she always has to be part of our sleepovers there. It's like having a huge tub of Cookie Dough ice-cream and finding a maggot in the middle of it.

"Look, my pathetic sister is NOT going to spoil things for us," said Kenny loudly. "We'll strap her on to the Wheel of Fear at the fair, lock her in the bathroom when we have our midnight feast, and she is absolutely NOT coming to our picnic in the park on Sunday."

Just then, Emily Berryman walked past with her nose in the air as usual. Emma Hughes was right behind her. I swear that those two must be joined by a piece of elastic, because one never goes anywhere without the other.

"Sounds like the babies have another of their exciting sleepovers planned. *And* going for a picnic in the park, too. How childish!" snorted one M&M, just loud enough for us to hear.

"It's time they grew up and did more mature

things like us, isn't it?" sneered the other one.

"Yeah, sure, like prancing about in front of a mirror and telling each other how wonderful we are," snarled Kenny. "Get a life!"

As they were walking away, a group of little girls came pirouetting around the corner and bumped straight into the M&Ms, nearly knocking them over.

"Oh, it's you!" snapped Emma Hughes to one poor girl. "If you were as good at dancing as you think you are, you would be able to see where you were going!" The little girl went bright red, her eyes filled with tears and she hurried away.

"Are you all right?" Fliss called after her.

"That's one of my brother's friends," she explained to the rest of us. "I think it's a bit much when the M&Ms are so nasty to a six-year-old. What has she ever done to them?"

Emma Hughes ignored Fliss and said to Emily Berryman, "There are just too many babies round here, aren't there?" And they both sniggered as they walked away.

When they had gone, Kenny said, "One day I swear that I'm going to teach those two a lesson."

Of course, we believed her. We just didn't realise how soon that day would come!

I was so excited when I got home that evening. I was

just planning what to wear for the 24-hour sleepover when the phone rang.

"It's that crazy friend of yours, Frankie," Dad called upstairs. That had to be Kenny. "Try not to hog the phone *all* night, will you?"

My dad thinks he's so funny, but I guess I do spend a long time gossiping on the phone.

I was going to ring you, Kenny. Do you think jeans and a crop top will be all right for the fair? And what are you going to wear for the picnic?

All I could hear at the other end of the line was a sort of sniffing.

That is you, isn't it, Kenny?

This time there were a few gulps among the sniffs.

Have you got some kind of disease?

*I can't have the 24-hour sleepover*, she sobbed.

What? Why?

*Dad's going to be away at some stupid conference and mum has promised to go and see my Aunty Mary in Norwich that weekend. I told Mum that we'd all stay here without them, but she went ballistic.*

I wonder why? I laughed; then I had

one of my brainwaves.

Hang on, Kenny. You can't have it at your house, but what's to stop me having the sleepover here?

*Your parents?*

Don't be daft, Kenny. This is Frankie you're speaking to, not Fliss. I'll talk my parents round. Easy-peasy.

*Frankie, you're the best. See you tomorrow. And good luck!*

Am I clever or am I clever?

Of course, once I'd promised I had to come up with the goods, didn't I? So I went into the lounge where Mum and Dad were watching some boring television programme. I settled down on the settee between them and pretended that I was really interested in it, too.

"All right, Frankie, what do you want?" asked Dad.

"Well, I was just thinking," I said, very innocently. "If you had a friend who had invited you and some of his mates round for a weekend… "

"Y-es," said my dad, suspiciously.

"And then he found that for some reason he

couldn't use his *own* home that particular weekend, I wouldn't mind a bit if you all came here instead."

Mum let out a loud laugh.

"I'm sure you wouldn't," she said.

"And I was wondering… " I continued.

"You were wondering if you could invite your friends round here for your next sleepover. Right?" He's very quick, my dad.

"It's the 24-hour sleepover, actually," I reminded them.

They both groaned.

"Not the fair, anything but the fair," gasped Mum, pretending to collapse on the settee.

She loves it really, so does Dad. They went on more rides than we did last year.

"OK, OK. I think we can cope with the Fearless Five for 24 hours, don't you?" my dad said.

"Thanks, Dad, you're the greatest," I said, planting a big kiss on his forehead. I gave Mum a big hug and a kiss too and danced up to my room. I still had to decide what to wear for the picnic.

# CHAPTER TWO

I never actually got round to choosing my clothes for the picnic. Instead I made cute little Change of Sleepover Venue cards for the others.

> **A T T E N T I O N !**
> We have a **CHANGE OF VENUE** situation!
> The 24-hour sleepover
> on
> 👍 **SATURDAY 6TH JULY** 👍
> will now be held at
> **FRANKIE'S HOUSE**
> Usual sleepover rules apply!

Pretty neat or what?

We have so many sleepovers at each other's houses now that we never mind *where* we go. But having this one at my place did have one major advantage.

"No Molly The Monster!" shouted Lyndz and Fliss together when I handed them their change of venue cards.

"Yeah, she's in a real mood!" laughed Kenny. "It's wicked!"

"I didn't think she liked us coming to stay at your place," said Rosie.

"No, she doesn't, but she *was* looking forward to going to the fair. And now she can't because she's got to go to Norwich with Mum. One-nil!" shouted Kenny, leaping about as though Leicester City had just won the FA Cup!

"I see the babies are getting excited again," said Emma Hughes, who just happened to be stalking past us. "Have their mummies promised to take them to the fair, then?" She put on a really stupid, babyish voice.

"They'll have to remember to take some spare nappies," laughed her side-kick, Emily Berryman. "We all know what happens to babies when they get over-excited." They cackled like two constipated hyenas and ran away. It took me all my time to stop Kenny rushing after them. I hate to think what she would have done if I'd let her go.

"They're not worth it, Kenny," said Lyndz. "Try not to let them get to you."

"I can't help it," seethed Kenny, who was bright red in the face. "They just wind me up. I swear that I'm going to get even with them."

"Yeah, yeah, yeah," I said putting my arm round her shoulder. I'd heard the same thing since we were five and we hadn't exactly managed to get one over them yet.

Still, Kenny was my best friend and it was always wise to humour her.

"We'll think of something really gruesome," I said. "And then they'll be sorry they were born."

The whistle went for the start of school. We tried to hop all the way inside but Mrs Poole, the headmistress, screwed up her face and frowned at us. One of her looks could turn milk sour at ten paces. As soon as we saw her we walked normally into our classroom, then exploded into laughter. Apart from Fliss, of course. She was the colour of boiled beetroot. She just *hates* being told off, or, in this case, just looked at!

At break time we went to the studio to practise one of our dance routines. But when we got there, a group of young girls were already  clustered outside watching someone dancing. They were the same girls who we'd seen dancing in the playground the day before. We looked into the studio to see who they were watching. Wouldn't you know it, the stupid M&Ms had got there first.

"I don't believe it!" shouted Rosie. "They're starting to spoil all our fun."

"And they can't even dance properly!" smirked Lyndz.

"Somebody told me that the last time they took their dancing exams, a *six-year-old* got better grades than they did!" laughed Fliss. "Maybe those little girls are coaching them!"

We all laughed.

Inside the studio, Emma Hughes and Emily Berryman were thrashing about like flies caught in a cobweb. The music they were dancing to was some seriously gruesome classical number. Mum and Dad listen to a lot of classical stuff, and I actually quite like some of it, but this sounded like a couple of cats in a liquidiser!

"Do you suppose they're trying to do something from Swan Lake?" asked Rosie. "You know, dying swans and all that."

"I don't know about dying swans," snorted Kenny. "They look like dead ducks to me!"

The M&Ms must have heard us screaming with laughter, because they suddenly stopped dancing and started to stare at us.

"Uh-oh!" said Fliss. "I think it's time we went."

"No way!" snorted Kenny. "We've as much right to be here as they have."

Emma Hughes came over to the door. "Are you picking up a few tips?" she asked in her sickly-sweet voice. She was talking to us *and* the young girls. "I don't think there's any hope of *any* of *you* ever making the Royal Ballet School. The zoo might be interested in some fairy elephants though!"

We just laughed, but the little girls looked a bit upset.

"Well," sneered Kenny. "I'd rather be with some intelligent animals in a zoo than with sad no-hopers like you!"

"You're only jealous!" spat out Emily Berryman, who had come to join her friend at the studio door.

"Get a life!" we all shouted, and ran down the corridor.

After that, *Get a life!* became our way of greeting the M&Ms. And boy did they hate it! The joke did wear a bit thin after a while though. Then we turned our attention to the 24-hour sleepover again. I just couldn't wait!

You know when you're really, really looking forward to something, you just wish it was happening right now, don't you? The more you think about it, the more you want to close your eyes and sleep through all the days in between, and wake up and just start enjoying yourself. My gran says you shouldn't wish your life away and I suppose she's right. I do enjoy school and everything, but I was looking forward to the 24-hour sleepover so much, I just wanted it to be here, like NOW!

There were only ten days to go, anyway. We all made a sort of countdown in the back of our jotters. We wrote 10, 9, 8, 7, etc. down one side of the page and as each day went by we crossed off that number so we could see how many days we had left before the sleepover.

Rosie said that we really ought to write down something that had happened on each of the days we crossed off. A sort of miniature diary. This is what I wrote:

10. (WEDNESDAY)
MB&MS are getting worse. Nearly had World War III between them and Kenny today. Boy, is she getting mad!

9. (THURSDAY)
Had a good time at Brownies. Practised for the Sports Day in a couple of weeks time. Fliss kept tripping up. She was NOT happy!

8. (FRIDAY)
Had to read out poems in class. Mrs Weaver practically kissed Emma Hughes, because she said she read hers out with such feeling! BLAH! Pass the sick bucket!

7. (SATURDAY)
24-hour sleepover in a week's time — YIPPEE! Went shopping with Mum and Dad. Wouldn't buy me new shorts for the picnic. Major sulk. Took me for a pizza. They're not so bad after all!

**6 (SUNDAY)**
Homework. Bor-ing!
Kenny rang. On phone
for about three hours!
Dad nearly did his nut!

**5. (MONDAY)**
Last week at school
before the sleepover.
Kenny tripped up Emily
Berryman in PE. The
crybaby made such a
meal of it, you'd think
Kenny had done it on
purpose. Miss Burns tried
to calm things down,
but she's about as much
use as a chocolate
frying pan and just
made things worse. Fliss
is getting seriously
worried about Kenny.
She reckons she's getting
way too carried away
with this M&M feud
thing.

**4. (TUESDAY)**
Kenny put a spider in
Emma Hughes
lunchbox. She screamed
so much when she
found it, it sounded
like a horror movie.
The Day of The Crawling
Sandwich. I just hope
they don't find out
that Kenny did it,
because at the moment
she thinks she's won
their stupid feud.

**3. (Wednesday)**
The M&Ms did find out that Kenny was responsible for the spider incident. Today they tipped a jug of water all over Kenny's lunch. To make things worse, the kitchen had run out of the pie she was having and all they could give her was a plate full of swede! Poor Kenny.

**2. (Thursday)**
Lyndz made us all scream with laughter at Brownies. She hit a patch of mud in the field where we were practising for Sports Day. She tried to stop running but just kind of went on sliding. She ended up doing roly-polies all the way down the sloping bit of the field. She was laughing so much when she got up that tears were streaming down her face. Even Brown Owl couldn't stop laughing, once she'd made sure that Lyndz was all right.

**1. (Friday)**
ONE DAY TO GO! I can't believe that our 24-hour sleepover will be tomorrow!!! YIPPEE AND DOUBLE YIPPEE!!!

# CHAPTER THREE

The worst thing about our sleepovers is the hanging around waiting for them to start. It's all right for the others, they all have brothers and sisters. Don't get me started on that one, you must already know how I feel about being an only one. That's probably why I'm so bossy with the others in the Sleepover Club. I'm making up for all the times I should have been ordering people about at home! The others think I'm dead lucky having all the attention and stuff. I guess the grass *is* always greener on the other side, as my grandma says.

Anyway, this time the sleepover was going to

start early for me and Kenny. With her mum going away and everything, she was going to come to my house at lunchtime. Kenny always plays badminton on Saturday mornings, so her mum dropped her off at the badminton club on the way to her sister's in Norwich. Then she had arranged for my mum to collect Kenny from the club at twelve o'clock.

Mum and I waited inside the club and watched for a few minutes before they finished playing. Kenny was certainly thwacking the shuttlecocks around the court.

"You should do something like this, Frankie," said Mum looking on in admiration. "It might stop you moping around so much."

"Thanks, Mum, I *do not* mope around," I said crossly. "I play netball at school, anyway."

"Yes, but maybe you should do something like this on Saturdays. Ooh, good shot, Kenny!"

Once my mum gets something like that into her head, there's no stopping her. But she has obviously never seen me trying to hit something with a racket. Pathetic is not the word!

Kenny came flying off the court towards us.

"Kenny, I'm impressed!" said Mum. "What do you think about to get all that power behind your shots?"

Good old Mum, she always has to delve into these things. I think that's what being a lawyer does for you.

"Oh, that's easy," replied Kenny. "I just imagine that the shuttlecocks are the M&Ms' heads!"

That shut Mum up.

I couldn't believe it when it was almost five o'clock. I'd promised Mum that I would get my bedroom ready for the others as soon as we got back from collecting Kenny. But somehow we had got sidetracked. So we had a mad dash round, setting up the camp-bed and dusting down the bunk-beds.

Because there are five of us in the Sleepover Club now and only four beds, two of us usually have to share my bed. As Kenny is my best friend, and I'm used to her fidgeting about, it is usually her. Last time her feet were so freezing that I hardly got any sleep, so this time I insisted that we both sleep in our sleeping bags on the bed. And we decided that Lyndz might be safest in the bottom bunk, (after the camp-bed collapsed underneath her last time) with Fliss in the top one. Rosie is very sensible and

I didn't think she'd mind being on the camp-
bed.

We'd just about finished rearranging my
room for the sleepover when the doorbell
went.

"It's F-Time!" Kenny and I shouted together.
That is sleepover-speak for Fun Time, or the
start of our sleepover!

We dashed downstairs.

"You sound like a herd of elephants,"
shouted my dad. "I think I might charge people
to come round and look at you. Especially
when the rest of those wild animals you call
friends arrive."

We opened the door to find Fliss standing
there. She looked nothing at all like a wild
animal, more like a small mouse. She wiped her
feet about a million times, even though it
wasn't wet outside. Fliss's mum is very hot on
dirt. Getting rid of it that is. If she went on
*Mastermind*, her specialist subject would be
cleaning. And Fliss is going the same way.

"Fliss, for goodness' sake stop wiping your
feet and come in," I moaned. Kenny and I both
grabbed hold of one of her arms and almost
carried her upstairs. Even Fliss was laughing by
the time we had got to my room. We all flopped

down on my bed.

"Oh no!" gasped Fliss, delving into her rucksack. "I think this lemonade's going to explode!"

She pulled out a plastic bottle which was mainly full of cloudy bubbles. Kenny rushed over to the window with it, flung it open and unscrewed the bottle top. A fountain of liquid shot out.

"Oi! Watch it!" shouted a voice below. Fliss, Kenny and I all peeped out of the window. The lemonade had shot out all over Lyndz who was just walking up to the front door! I thought I was going to wet myself laughing. Lyndz just creased up, too. She was in a sort of crumpled heap on the doorstep when Dad opened it.

"I might have known it was you, Lyndsey," said Dad in his mock-headmaster's voice. "Oh no, not the hiccups. Please tell me you haven't got the hiccups already!"

Lyndsey is famous for her hiccups, but she doesn't usually get them so early in the sleepover. She gulped a few times and shook her head. We were spared them – for the moment.

"Thank goodness for that!" said my dad, patting his heart in fake relief. "OK, I think you'd all better give me your goodies for the midnight feast and tomorrow's picnic. I'm not sure that I can cope with any more edible explosions. Frankie's room is a big enough tip as it is!"

"Ha, ha, ha!" I said, handing over Fliss's bag of food. Lyndz gave him hers. Kenny's and, of course, mine were already in the kitchen.

Lyndz came upstairs and threw her stuff on the bottom bunk. While Dad had been teasing her in the hall, we had had time to prepare a squishy-poo. We stuffed all our sleepover clothes into my sleeping bag and then, when Lyndz's back was turned, we caught her unawares with it. She collapsed on to her bed in a fit of giggles. Her face was buried in her own sleeping bag which she had just put out. It wasn't long before we saw the unmistakeable shaking of her shoulders and a muffled *Hic* emerging from the bed.

"Oh Lyndz, you can't have hiccups now!" laughed Fliss.

There was nothing for it but my thumb-in-the-hand routine. We were so busy dealing with Lyndz that we didn't hear the doorbell go. And it wasn't until Rosie suddenly flew into the room, flushed and breathless, that we realised she had arrived.

"You'll never guess who I've just seen!" she shouted excitedly.

"Brad Pitt?" I asked.

"Was it all of Boyzone in the nude?" asked Lyndz, her hiccups having suddenly stopped.

"Emile Heskey?" asked Kenny excitedly. "You know, the Leicester City footballer," she added, as if we didn't know!

"No, stupids," said Rosie, dancing about on the spot. "I've just seen the M&Ms prancing about in a couple of tutus! They must have been going to some dumb old fancy-dress party!"

"And they said *we* were babyish for having sleepovers," snorted Kenny. "I'd just love to see them prancing about. That would wipe those stupid smiles off their faces!"

Fliss looked a bit puzzled.

"You know, I think *I've* seen them somewhere dressed like that," she said.

"Maybe that's their idea of fun on a Saturday night," laughed Lyndz. "They probably say to each other, 'Now what shall we do tonight? I know, let's dress up as ballerinas again!' "

The rest of us collapsed into fits of giggles.

"Come on, girls," shouted Kenny, pirouetting around the room. "Let's pretend *we're* ballet dancers!"

We all joined in, crashing into each other like a herd of hippopotamuses.

There was a knock on the door and Dad walked in.

"Oh no!" he gasped. "It's happened, hasn't it? You've been possessed by aliens!"

Mum came to stand in the doorway next to him.

"Oh, that's too bad," she sighed. "Just when I was going to tell them it was time we were getting ready to go to the fair!"

"Yes!" we all screamed.

And, of course, that's where the trouble really started.

# CHAPTER FOUR

It always takes forever for us to get ready to go out. You would think that we could just go out as we are. Wrong! We have to change about a million times, even though we hardly have any stuff to change into. We borrow each others' things, try on different combinations and end up wearing what we had intended to wear from the start! Then of course there's our hair to deal with!

Fliss is actually pretty great at doing different hairstyles. I think she must get it from her mum, who is a beautician. It's the one time when Fliss has lots of patience – she'll sit for hours doing our hair. And she's pretty cool at putting on make-up, too. When I think about it, I give Fliss a hard time about being a wimp and everything, but she's pretty great in other ways. And, let's be honest, the rest of us sometimes look like a dog's breakfast if we try to put make-up on ourselves.

Kenny, of course, is just not interested in all that stuff, and she started to get really ratty with us all for taking so long. She just wanted to go to the fair and go on all the scary rides!

Dad was getting a bit cross, too. "Come on girls!" he shouted upstairs. "Sometime this year would be good!"

Eventually we all piled downstairs.

"I think there must be some mistake," said Dad when he saw us. "It was my daughter and her friends I was waiting for. Who are you?"

He's crazy, my dad, but we all felt pretty flattered. We did look kind of cool and we felt grown-up with a bit of make-up on and our hair done differently.

We piled into the back of our estate car and sang along to the Spice Girls all the way into Leicester. Mum and Dad joined in the singing, too, but we tried to ignore them.

When we got to the fair, Dad parked in a muddy car park and we all scrambled out.

"Hey, not so fast you lot!" shouted Mum. "I know that you're all cool and don't want us old fuddy-duddies to cramp your style, but we want to know where you're going and we want you in our sight all the time. Is that understood?"

"Yes," we all sighed.

The air smelt of fried onions and petrol. The further we got into the fair, the more it smelt. And then there was the sickly-sweet smell of candyfloss, too. Anywhere else those smells would have turned my stomach. But because it was at the fair and had the accompaniment of loud music and flashing lights on all the rides, it actually smelt pretty good at the time. The whole thing was exciting.

We made our way over to the far side of the fairground to the Dungeon of Doom. It's just about the scariest thing at the fair so we usually do it first while it's still light. Then if we're feeling *really* brave before we go home, we do it again, in the dark.

"Last one there's a stewed prune!" yelled Kenny, charging towards the entrance. Lyndz and Rosie ran after her, screaming. I grabbed hold of Fliss's hand and started running, too.

"Come on, Fliss, we don't want to be stewed prunes, do we?"

Fliss laughed nervously. Fliss is dead squeamish, and last year she wouldn't come in with us. She hovered around outside and then made us all feel guilty for leaving her. It's always awful if one of us gets left out of things, like Rosie being left out of the netball team. But it *is* usually Fliss's choice not to join in. Anyway, I was determined that she was not going to spoil this sleepover by moaning.

"Come on, Fliss. It'll be a laugh. We'll all be there together. And it's not *that* scary really," I said.

Fliss had that set look on her face. She just nodded and said, "OK".

Mum hurtled past us from nowhere and dashed up to the entrance of the Dungeon of Doom, where Kenny, Lyndz and Rosie were waiting for us.

"Mum, what are you like!" I gasped when Fliss and I had run to join them. "Fancy being worried that you were going to be last at your age. You do embarrass me sometimes!"

Anyway, we eventually walked up a very steep flight of stairs inside the Dungeon of Doom. It was pitch black. I could hear lots of squealing somewhere in the distance. Then I felt a hand grab my throat.

"Is that you Frankie?" hissed Fliss.

I struggled free.

"Yes, but it was nearly a dead Frankie. You nearly strangled me!" I choked.

"Sorry," she squeaked. "I'm scared. I want to go out."

"No way are you leaving now," I told her. "Look, just grab hold of my arm and when we get used to the dark we should be able to see a bit more."

We stood still, holding on to each other. I could hear Kenny shrieking somewhere in front of me.

"Are you OK, Kenny?" I shouted.

"I've just trodden in something that feels like a mass of eyeballs," she shouted back. "It's brill!"

"I'm going, Frankie, I don't like this!" squeaked Fliss.

"Look, just follow me," I said.

We shuffled along very slowly. Then suddenly we hit a sort of moving treadmill.

"You've got to run on this until it stops," I told Fliss.

She screamed a bit, but she seemed OK really. When it stopped we went into a room where the air got colder and it felt kind of damp. Suddenly a gush of water shot down the wall behind us and splashed our clothes.

"This is not fun!" wailed Fliss. "I want to go ho... o... o... me!"

She suddenly disappeared.

"Are you all right, Fliss?" I called.

"No," came a little voice which sounded as if it was coming from the bottom of a well.

My eyes were getting more used to the dark now and I could just make out a hole in the floor which was attached to a chute. It must have led to the floor below.

"Hang on Fliss! I'm coming down," I called.

Just as I was about to jump down the chute, I heard someone behind me.

"Oh this is just gross! I'm completely soaked. I wish I hadn't worn these new jeans."

"I know," said another voice. "It's so dark in here, I hope we don't break our legs or anything. Then we'd miss out on all the fun in the park tomorrow!"

It was the M&Ms! I was sure it was. I'd recognise Emily Berryman's gruff voice anywhere. I couldn't wait to tell the others.

When I got to the bottom of the chute, Fliss was still in a crumpled heap. Rosie was with her. She had slid down a fireman's pole. Kenny and Lyndz were still running wild on the upper floor. We could hear their screaming and giggling from where we were.

"You'll never guess who I've just heard," I said, pulling Fliss to her feet.

"Oasis?" asked Rosie hopefully.

"Nope. The M&Ms. They were upstairs."

"I thought you said they were going to a fancy-dress party," Fliss said to Rosie.

"I thought they were. They were all dressed up, anyway."

"Maybe they thought you should dress like fairies to come to the fair!" laughed Fliss.

Fliss *never* makes jokes. And that one was actually quite funny.

"That's very good, Fliss!" said Rosie, and we all laughed. Fliss looked very pleased with herself. She even seemed to forget what an awful time she'd had in the Dungeon of Doom.

"Are you sure it was them? What did they say?" asked Rosie when we had calmed down.

"Well I couldn't see them," I admitted. "But one of them was complaining about wearing new jeans. The other said it was too dark. And something about hoping they didn't break their legs because they didn't want to miss the fun in the park tomorrow."

"They're not coming to our picnic are they?" asked Fliss.

"Of course not," I snorted.

"Maybe it wasn't them at all, Frankie," said Rosie.

I was about to disagree when something

charged into me. Kenny and Lyndsey had both come crashing down the chute, one after the other. They were both helpless with laughter.

"That was wicked!" gasped Kenny. "Let's do it again!"

"Let's not," moaned Fliss. "Let's go and get some candyfloss. I'm hungry!"

We all groaned. We were all hungry too. But not for candyfloss. That must be the biggest let-down known to humanity. It always *sounds* nice, but after a couple of mouthfuls you realise it burns your tongue, it's too sickly and you're left holding the stupid stuff for the rest of the evening. Fliss loves it.

We trooped over to the part of the fair where the food stalls were. Fliss bought her candyfloss, the others had hot dogs and Mum, Dad and I had a cheese pancake each.

Kenny is the messiest eater known to mankind. So it was no surprise when she squirted tomato ketchup all down her prized Leicester City top.

"Oh rats!" she shouted, trying to scrape off the gloopy liquid.

We were all dabbing her and rubbing at the marks, when who should strut past? Yep, you've guessed it, the M&Ms!

# CHAPTER FIVE

Oh yes, the M&Ms. We were all fussing round Kenny when they walked past. They looked pretty stupid actually, done up like a couple of Barbies in lots of make-up, new jeans and high heels. I mean, who in their right mind would go to a fair in a muddy field in *high heels*? Or, as Kenny said, who in their right mind would wear high heels with jeans anyway!

But the thing was that they were there by themselves, thinking they looked so cool. And there were we, fussing around Kenny as though she was a toddler, with *my parents* hovering in the background! Dorksville!

As soon as the others saw them too, we all kind of went on to automatic pilot. Rosie clamped her hand over Lyndz's mouth, and Fliss did the same to Kenny. If anyone was going to show us up, it would be those two. I stooped over as far as I could without injuring myself. My height always gives me away. I tend to look like a giraffe in a field full of horses. We huddled together as much as possible, and held our breath.

The M&Ms walked right by us and never said a thing. They seemed more concerned about the splashes of mud which were creeping up their jeans.

"Who were they?" asked Mum and Dad when the coast was clear.

"The M&Ms!" we all shrieked together.

"They look older than I do!" muttered Mum.

"Yeah right, Mum! You wish!" I laughed, but I knew what she meant.

"Don't ever think you're going out looking like that," Dad suddenly said to me quite sternly. "There's plenty of time for dressing up when you're older."

"Chill out, Dad!" I said. "Why would I *want* to look like that anyway?"

"Do you think they saw us?" asked Fliss.

"Nah," said Kenny, still rubbing at the patch of ketchup on her shirt. "They would have said something."

"Maybe Frankie's parents put them off," said Fliss anxiously.

"Thank you very much, Fliss!" laughed Mum.

Fliss went bright red. "I didn't mean… " she mumbled.

"Oh Fliss, I was only joking," said Mum.

"I thought you said you saw them in their tutus," Kenny said to Rosie. She didn't know that I'd heard them in the Dungeon of Doom already.

"Yes, I did," admitted Rosie. "Maybe they changed their minds about the party. Or maybe they'd just been dressing up, like we do sometimes."

We agreed that even the M&Ms could do normal things like that.

"Right then, who's for the dodgems?" shouted Mum.

She and Dad raced over to the cars. I told you that they enjoy the fair more than we do. Kenny went in a dodgem by herself. She drives like a madwoman so nobody ever wants to go with her. Rosie and Fliss went together and I went in a car with Lyndz.

Mum and Dad were just about the worst drivers there, and kept pinning us all into corners.

"Hi, sis!" shouted a voice in our direction. It was gorgeous Tom, one of Lyndz's brothers.

"You women drivers are all the same!" he laughed as he shot past, in hot pursuit of a pouting blonde in another dodgem.

"I might have known my stupid brother would be here!" said Lyndz. "I expect the others are causing chaos somewhere. They had better stay out of my way! I want *one* night on my own without them."

You see! Those people who have brothers and sisters don't want them, and those who haven't, do. It's a funny old world, as my grandma says.

After the dodgems, we went on the Wheel of Fear. You probably know it already. You're strapped into a sort of cage in a wheel and it spins faster and faster until you don't know which way up you are. Fliss gave that one a miss. She said it made her feel sick just looking at it!

"Isn't that Callum over there?" asked Rosie. Callum is Fliss's brother.

"Where?" asked Fliss, spinning round.

We all looked to where Rosie was pointing. Sure enough, there was Callum with the pretty girl who had danced into the M&Ms in the playground. They were holding hands.

"Oh yuk, how embarrassing!" laughed Fliss, pretending to be sick. "He's with his girlfriend. And those must be her parents." She pointed to the couple who were walking right behind them. I should remind you that Callum is only seven.

"Ah! Sweet!" we laughed.

"Must be *lurve* if they've come to the fair together!" said Kenny, pretending to go all gooey.

"Oh, but they do everything together," said Fliss. "It's really weird. She goes to her dancing class on Saturdays, so Callum said that he wanted to go too. Now he actually goes *dancing* with her. Can you imagine? There's just him and about twenty girls."

"It looks as though they've brought the rest of the dancing class with them as well!" laughed Dad.

We looked over to see Callum now surrounded by about eight little girls all giggling and twirling. He was the only boy, but he didn't seem to mind.

We all spluttered with laughter.

"Well I think it's very sweet of Callum," said

Mum.

"I think it's kind of sweet, too," agreed Fliss. "But he's going to perform in some kind of concert with them tomorrow. Talk about embarrassing! I'm just glad that I'm going on the picnic with you lot. I'd *die* if I had to watch him prancing about in a pair of tights!"

"Oh I don't know, it might be a laugh," said Kenny. "Let's go and watch him!"

"No way!" shouted Fliss. "We are not going to see my brother making a fool of himself. And that's final!"

She sounded as though she meant it, too.

"OK, OK. Keep your hair on!" snapped Kenny.

"We haven't been on the Ghost Train yet," yelled Lyndz. "Come on!"    Lyndz is amazing. She always knows how to stop arguments escalating into World War III.

Kenny, Rosie and I charged after her like a herd of stampeding buffalo. Fliss hung back with Mum and Dad. I stopped running and shouted to her, "Come on Fliss! The Ghost Train wouldn't frighten anybody. Honest!"

"It's OK. I think Fliss would rather stay with us," Mum said, running up to me. "And I don't think your father can cope with any more excitement either! Look, here's the money for the four of you and we'll wait for you at the end."

I ran on to join the others. I paid for us all. Then we had to queue up a short ramp to wait for the train. As we shuffled forward, the ramp became darker and darker, until we couldn't even see each other.

"This is so lame!" I heard Kenny complaining. But I could tell by the sound of her voice that she was just the teeniest bit scared. There was something about the musty smell which hung in the air that made it feel sort of creepy.

When it was our turn to climb on to the train, Kenny and Lyndz squashed into the front seat of one carriage and Rosie and I got into the seat behind. It was so dark that you couldn't see the next carriage at all.

As the train started to rumble through the doors, cobwebs hung down and brushed our faces. Kenny screamed and Lyndz started to giggle. That started me and Rosie off.

"I dare you to touch one of those skeletons," Rosie whispered to me. She pointed to a group of them swinging next to the train. As we passed them, I leaned out to shake one of their hands. I couldn't believe it when its *whole arm* came off! I screamed so hard, I thought my lungs would burst.

"Francesca Theresa Thomas!" boomed Kenny in her 'Mrs Weaver' voice. "Do calm down!"

Of course, we all cracked up with laughter. And that's when the train stopped.

Everybody screamed. But really it wasn't too much of a surprise because it happens every year. "This is so childish, I don't know why we came."

That just had to be Emily Berryman. I nudged Rosie to listen too and we both turned round. It was very dark in the tunnel. But even if it had been lit up like Blackpool illuminations we wouldn't have been able to see who was in the carriage behind us. It had stopped round a bend in the tunnel. So whoever the speaker was, she was hidden from us.

"I know, but it's good to see what our little baby friends get up to for fun. And we've already seen how much they're enjoying the fair. Giggling and laughing like that. It's probably the most exciting thing they've ever done in their lives!" Rosie and I clutched each other's arms. There was no mistaking Emma Hughes' voice.

"Fancy having to be chaperoned by your

parents!" laughed one M&M. "But I suppose they are only young!" They both started giggling.

"They're talking about us! They must have seen us!" spluttered Rosie. "The cheek of it! They're only a few months older than any of us."

I was getting mad, I don't mind telling you. Who did they think they were? But then it got worse.

"I can't stand that Laura," whined Emma Hughes. "She's always got her stupid little friends round her. It's like she thinks she's some sort of goddess. Well I'm going to get my own back on her in the park tomorrow! There's no way she'll try to mess with me again!"

They must have been talking about Kenny. Laura's her real name but she hates it. The M&Ms are always calling her Laura because they know that it winds her up. But I really couldn't believe that Kenny ever thought of herself as a *goddess*. She'd rather die! *And* I hadn't realised that Kenny had got to Emma Hughes that much. But if she was talking about getting her own back, then Kenny must have upset her more than we thought.

Anyway, Kenny is my best mate and I wasn't

going to let anyone slag her off. I made a move to get out of the carriage to go and tell those stupid M&Ms exactly what I thought of them. But Rosie held me back. She put her finger to her lips. The M&Ms were still talking.

"We should prove to ALL of them that we're better than they are. I think showing them up in public is just what they need!" They both started cackling like a couple of witches.

"Oh no! They're going to do something to us at the picnic tomorrow!" squeaked Rosie. "We'll have to warn the others."

We leaned forward to tell Kenny and Lyndz but they weren't there. They had disappeared!

# CHAPTER SIX

Rosie and I couldn't believe it. Where on earth could Kenny and Lyndz have gone?

"You don't suppose the Ghost Train really is haunted do you?" asked Rosie. She is usually very calm, but I could see that she was starting to panic.

"You mean ghosts have come and spirited Kenny and Lyndz away?" I said. "Come on Rosie. Who in their right mind would get involved with either of those two? You know what chaos they always cause when they're together."

"Yeah, you're right," she laughed. "Nobody would be crazy enough to mess with Kenny and Lyndz. They'd be enough to frighten any ghost!"

Suddenly a strange, spooky sort of noise filled the tunnel. It sounded like a ghoulish moaning. Rosie and I clung to each other. We could hear the M&Ms screaming behind us. Then another, louder groan seemed to shake the train carriages.

"I think there really must be a ghost!" whispered Rosie. I could feel her trembling beside me.

"Oh come on Rosie! You know that there are no such things as ghosts," I said, trying to sound brave. "It's probably a recording that they put on when the train stops."

"It sounded real enough to me," mumbled Rosie, shivering. She was digging her fingernails hard into my arm.

"Ouch, Rosie. I think you're piercing a vein there," I complained.

"Sorry," she said quietly.

A shriek echoed round the tunnel walls. Everybody started to scream again. Even me! My heart was pounding and I felt as though I couldn't breathe.

"Do you *still* say there aren't any ghosts?" demanded Rosie. She was squeezing my arm harder than before.

But then something convinced me once and

for all that this was no ghost we were dealing with. The unmistakeable sound of giggling, accompanied by a loud *Hic!* bounced around the tunnel walls.

"Kenny and Lyndz!" Rosie and I mouthed to each other.

"Come on, let's go and find them!" I yelled, leaping out of the carriage.

The sound of their giggling had come from somewhere behind all the cobwebs and ghosts which were flapping about beside the track.

"BOO!"

Kenny and Lyndz suddenly popped out from behind the skeletons. Rosie and I laughed so much I thought we were going to wet ourselves.

"Look! We found a microphone hidden back here," Kenny shouted. "They must use it for making announcements. Did you like our sound effects? Good, hah?"

"No, they were not good, you young villains," boomed a voice behind us.

We spun round to see a very angry, red-faced man heading towards us. It was the owner of the Ghost Train ride.

"How dare you tamper with private property! I've a good mind to call the police!"

We stopped laughing when he said that.

"Now get out, all of you. And don't you dare come back on this ride ever again!"

He pushed us towards a door marked Emergency Exit and we all stumbled out into the fresh air. We heard the Ghost Train start to rumble inside the building again. Suddenly Rosie remembered our news.

"Hey, you'll never guess what we heard in the Ghost Train!" she said excitedly.

"Erm, let me guess. Could it have been... *Oooooooh*..." Kenny started to moan and groan.

"No stupid, something much more exciting than that," I said.

"Oh thanks very much. I thought I was rather good, actually," grumbled Kenny.

"Oh shut up and listen, will you!" I shouted. "This is really important."

"Yes, we heard the M&Ms – and they're going to sabotage our picnic tomorrow!" blurted out Rosie.

"No way!" shouted Lyndz. Her hiccups seemed to have stopped.

"Yes way!" I said. "Come on, let's find Fliss. We ought to get home to start planning our revenge!"

Mum and Dad couldn't believe it when we met them and insisted that we went home straight away.

"Aw, that's not fair!" moaned Fliss. "You've been on more rides than me."

"Yes well, whose choice was that?" I asked crossly.

"Francesca!" Mum reprimanded me.

"I'm sorry, Fliss," I said. I was sorry too, but sometimes she winds me up, always moaning about things not being fair.

"We've got some news," Rosie told Fliss. "And believe me, when you've heard it, you won't bother about missing a few rides. Anyway, you've got a furry octopus and we haven't."

I was impressed. Rosie had made Fliss smile again.

"I hope you're not going to be hatching one of your silly plans," Dad said in his stern lawyer's voice.

"Course not, Dad, what do you take us for?" I lied.

In my room we all flopped down on the bed.

"OK, what have I missed?" demanded Fliss.

"Well, me and Lyndz did this brilliant thing.

55

We got off the Ghost Train and made lots of spooky noises and Frankie and Rosie found us and then we got thrown out!" spluttered Kenny.

"You mean that's it?" yelled Fliss. "You dragged me home just to tell me that I've missed all the fun. Some friends you are!"

"Calm down, Fliss!" said Rosie. "What we wanted to tell you was that whilst those two were acting like Bart Simpson, Frankie and I heard the M&Ms. They must have been sitting behind us on the Ghost Train. Anyway, they're going to try to do something to us at our picnic tomorrow!"

"*What*?" screeched Fliss. "How do you know? What did they say? Did they threaten you or something?"

"No, nothing like that," I admitted. "They didn't even know we were there. We just overheard them going on about the babies having to be chaperoned at the fair."

"They must have been talking about us," Rosie butted in, "because that's what they always call us these days."

"Yes, and they said that Laura was the worst," I continued, "and that they were going to teach us *all* a lesson tomorrow."

"Laura?" shrieked Kenny. "I hate it when

they call me that! Anyway, you never told me that they mentioned me in particular. What did they say?" Her face was getting redder and redder. Kenny is not a pretty sight when she's angry. I looked to Rosie for assistance.

"Well," she said slowly, "I can't remember exactly. It was something about you thinking you're a goddess!"

Lyndz laughed so hard I thought she was going to choke.

"A goddess!" she spluttered. "Kenny a goddess! Do me a favour! When was the last time you saw a picture of a goddess wearing a football shirt?"

"That's not the point!" yelled Kenny. "What did they mean? They were saying I'm soft, weren't they? I'll show them!"

"Calm down, Kenny! Maybe we got that bit wrong," I said. "What Emma Hughes *did* say was that she was going to get her own back on you. So something you've done must have got her worried." Kenny cheered up a bit when she heard that.

"The most important thing is how are we going to stop them sabotaging our picnic?" I asked the others.

"We could give the park a miss and go

somewhere else," suggested Fliss. "Then they won't be able to do anything to us because we won't be there."

"That's typical of you," snapped Kenny. "You always run away because you're so terrified of doing anything wrong. I don't know why we even let you become a member of the Sleepover Club in the first place!"

We all went quiet. What Kenny had just said was true. Not the bit about her being a member of the Sleepover Club. The bit about Fliss running away. When the going gets tough, Fliss gets going in the opposite direction! But hearing somebody say it out loud somehow made it sound so much worse. It was like a big hairy spider that we'd been keeping in a box. Once it was let out in the open, it was impossible to ignore it.

Fliss went very pink and tears welled up in her eyes.

"Kenny! That wasn't very nice," said Lyndz crossly.

Rosie already had her arm around Fliss's shoulder. "Are you all right?" she asked gently.

It was awful. We are always having disagreements within the Sleepover Club, but this was different somehow.

"I'll go then, shall I?" mumbled Fliss. She made an effort to get up from the bed, but we all pulled her back down again. All of us except Kenny.

"Don't be stupid Fliss. How could we have a sleepover without you?" I asked. Fliss sort of smiled through her tears.

Kenny glowered. She knew that she was in the wrong, but sometimes she finds it hard to admit.

"I know that I'm not as brave as the rest of you… " said Fliss.

Kenny snorted.

"…but I can't help it," Fliss started to cry again.

"Look Fliss," I said, "my gran always says that it takes all sorts to make a world. We're all different and that's probably why we all get along so well. Usually."

"Why don't you just say sorry, Kenny?" asked Lyndz, who is always the peacemaker. "Then we can get back to the fun. This is supposed to be out special sleepover."

We all glared at Kenny. We had looked forward to the sleepover for so long, and now it looked as though it was all going to end in tears.

"OK, I'm sorry," mumbled Kenny. Fliss just nodded but she still seemed very upset.

"Do you know what I'm thinking?" asked Rosie.

"Er yes, like we've all suddenly become mind-readers!" I laughed. I was desperate to lighten things up again.

"I was just thinking that the M&Ms have probably got what they wanted.They would have loved it if they'd seen us all falling out with each other because of them." We all nodded.

"Yes, you're right! Give the girl a banana!" I said. "What we need now is a cunning plan to sort them out once and for all!"

"But first we should have a pillow fight to get rid of all our aggression," suggested Lyndz. "And I think Fliss should use a squishy-poo to get back at Kenny!" Fliss stopped crying and wiped her tears away with the back of her hand. Her face was all red and blotchy, but at least she was smiling again.

Before we knew what was happening, Fliss had swung her squishy-poo behind her head and thwacked Kenny so hard with it that she crumpled on to the floor.

We all stared at her in horror. Kenny wasn't moving.

# CHAPTER SEVEN

"Oh my God, Kenny, are you all right?" I gasped, kneeling beside her on the floor.

"I've killed her, haven't I?" wailed Fliss. "I didn't mean to. I've killed her and I'll have to go to prison." She started to sob again. Loud, miserable sobs.

"Don't be stupid, Fliss, of course you haven't killed her!" said Rosie sternly. "But maybe you ought to get your parents, Frankie, just in case."

Fliss began to howl again. I could hear Mum and Dad coming up the stairs. They must have heard all the noise. My heart started to pound. They would *never* let me have another sleepover after this.

Lyndz meanwhile had straddled Kenny's body.

"I've seen them do this on the telly," she said, and slapped Kenny hard around her face a couple of times.

"Oi!" yelled Kenny, struggling to get free of Lyndz. "I was only pretending. There's no need to get nasty!" She had gone very red in the face, but she was laughing. She and Lyndz were rolling around on the floor in a play-fight when Mum and Dad burst into my room.

"What on earth is going on in here?" asked my dad.

Kenny and Lyndz stopped ripping chunks out of each other and scrambled to their feet.

"Didn't I tell you not to get hyper?" said Mum in her weary, I-knew-this-would-happen tone of voice.

"It always ends in tears, doesn't it?" grumbled Dad looking from Fliss to me.

"I'm all-all right," stammered Fliss. "I didn't mean to… "

"She didn't mean to make you rush upstairs like that," I said quickly. "She's still a bit excited after the fair, aren't you, Fliss?"

Fliss nodded. Mum and Dad looked very

doubtful.

"Well, maybe it's time you thought about settling down for the night," said Mum.

"And if we have to come upstairs to you again," continued Dad, "you won't be having another sleepover until you're all collecting your pensions!"

"OK, Dad," I said as sweetly as I could. "We promise to be good." The others all nodded.

"All right, then. Well hurry up and get ready for bed," said Dad. "I know you lot. You're the world experts on taking as long as possible to get into bed! You could go on lecture tours abroad, present television programmes on the subject... " His voice faded as he closed the door behind him. When we had heard Mum and Dad go downstairs, we all let out a huge sigh.

"Thanks, Frankie!" moaned Fliss. "I bet your parents think I'm a real wimp. *Still excited after the fair!* You made me sound like a five-year-old!"

I could see Kenny narrowing her eyes and staring at Fliss. That wasn't a good sign. I couldn't go through all that shouting and crying again.

"I'm sorry, Fliss, it's all I could think of," I admitted.

"Look, we're all friends again and that's what matters," said Lyndz, grabbing us all in a group hug.

"But you know what?" asked Kenny, when she had managed to struggle free. "We've still got to sort out what we're going to do about those stupid M&Ms tomorrow."

In all the chaos, I'd almost forgotten about them.

"OK, well let's get ready for bed first," I suggested. "We usually do our best thinking when we're in bed."

The others agreed, so we got our nightclothes out of our bags and started to get undressed. As this was a sleepover, we did our invisible striptease inside our sleeping bags. It wasn't easy for me because Kenny's sleeping bag was next to mine on my bed. She's like a ferret caught in a sack sometimes. Her arms and legs were thrashing about. She almost pushed me off the bed twice!

"You look like an escapologist!" laughed Rosie. She had already changed into her pyjamas and was watching Kenny's performance.

"Hey, maybe that's what we could do!" shrieked Lyndz. "We could grab the M&Ms, tie them up, take them somewhere really spooky and leave them to untie themselves."

"Earth to Lyndsey!" I said. "This is the real world you know, not some spooky film. We want to teach them a lesson, not end up on *Crimewatch*. It's got to be something simple that will make them look stupid. Nobody has to know that we're involved."

Fliss looked relieved.

"Couldn't we just send them a nasty letter?" she asked. "We could write it on your computer, Frankie."

"No, I think it needs more than a letter, Fliss," said Rosie. "If they're planning to do something to us on our picnic tomorrow, we've got to get in with our plan first."

We all trooped off to the bathroom with our toilet bags. None of us enjoys washing much, so we never take much time doing that. But it's amazing how long it takes for five of us to do everything else you need to do before going to bed.

"And here we have the dawdling about by the bathroom technique... " Mum suddenly appeared as the rest of us were waiting for Fliss to finish brushing her teeth.

"And what is your advice to those girls who are worried about not taking long enough over their bedtime wash?" she asked Kenny, thrusting a pretend microphone in front of her face.

"Aw, give it a rest Mum" I pleaded. "We're going as fast as we can. You want us to be clean, don't you?"

"I don't care about clean, my girl," Mum laughed. "I just want you lot tucked up in bed!"

Fliss appeared out of the bathroom and did a twirl in her nightdress.

"I'm done!" she shouted. She didn't realise that Mum was there.

"I'm very pleased to hear it, Felicity," she said. "You're a sensible girl. Will you *please* get the rest of them to go to bed!"

When we got back to my room, we all snuggled down in our sleeping bags and got out our diaries.

"Why don't we all write down what we think we should do to the M&Ms and then vote on the best idea?" suggested Fliss.

Fliss is very keen on voting for things. We all thought her idea was a good one though, so we started thinking up our plans. The thing was, it was harder to write anything down than I had imagined. I knew that I wanted to get even with the M&Ms. And I knew that, more than anything, I didn't want them to do anything awful to us. That was a point of honour. But I just couldn't think of anything sensible that we could do to them. The harder I tried to think, the more my mind went blank.

"I can't really think of anything," I admitted.

"Me neither," agreed Lyndz.

"I've just written: *Send a nasty letter saying we'll see them in the park. Then we go somewhere else,*" said Fliss.

We all groaned.

"Well at least I *did* try," moaned Fliss. "And they would feel stupid if they turned up and we weren't there."

"That's true," I admitted. "But I think we've got to take more positive action. I mean really *do* something to the M&Ms."

"I'm not so sure about this," whined Fliss. "There's something not quite right about us attacking the M&Ms in public!"

"Oh don't start again!" shouted Kenny. "Would you rather they attacked us?" Fliss shook her head.

"But Fliss, we're not going to be actually *fighting* with the M&Ms or anything. We don't do that," I reassured her. Kenny looked disappointed.

"Besides," I continued, "we've had run-ins with the M&Ms for as long as we've been at school. You've never minded before. What's changed now?"

"Well I have always minded a bit," admitted Fliss quietly. She looked as though she was going to cry again. "But this time there's something else."

"What?" we all asked together.

"I don't know," she shouted. "That's just it. There's something at the back of my mind telling me that this isn't such a good idea. But I just don't know what it is."

"Could it be that you're a wimp?" asked Kenny, innocently.

We all shot her a look. I would be in deep doom if Fliss and Kenny fell out again after what happened last time.

"What have *you* written anyway, Kenny?" asked Lyndz suddenly.

"I've written: *Wait for stinky stupid M&Ms by park gates; make sure we're hidden from them. When they walk past, leap out at them, cut off their stupid blonde hair, stuff it down their throats and…*"

"Er, Kenny, I think you're taking this a bit too seriously," I said, snatching her diary from her.

I read what else she'd written and, believe me, her suggestions got worse. Much worse.

"We only want to teach them a lesson," said Lyndz.

"OK then, clever clogs," said Kenny. "What did *you* come up with?"

"Well I didn't," admitted Lyndz. "It's harder than I thought."

We all agreed about that.

"I vote that we have a dance before we go to bed," I said. "You never know, it might give us inspiration."

I whacked my Spice cassette into the machine and we all started to dance. We were in mid-routine when Mum knocked on the door and came in.

"At this rate, you should have started getting ready for bed before we went to the fair!" she groaned. "Come on girls, I've had enough excitement for one day and I'm ready for bed myself. Into bed all of you. I'm going to turn out the light."

We scrambled into our sleeping bags.

"Night-night!" called Mum as she closed the door.

"Night-night!" we all called back.

We counted to twenty-five then turned on

our torches. We always put them next to our sleeping bags, so that we're prepared for lights out.

"What do you suppose the M&Ms will do to us?" asked Fliss. She sounded a bit anxious.

"I can't believe they'll do anything much," said Rosie. "They'll be too concerned about messing up their precious hair." We all laughed.

"I know one thing," said Lyndz, very seriously.

"What?" we all asked.

"I'm *starving*!" replied Lyndz, and burst out laughing. "It's all this concentrating!"

I had forgotten to bring the goodies upstairs with me when we got back from the fair. I wasn't sure that Mum and Dad would be thrilled about me going downstairs again, but what could I do? What is a sleepover without a midnight feast?

I crept out of bed and shone my torch over to the door.

"I'll be as quick as I can!" I whispered.

When I opened my bedroom door, something scrunchy fell on my foot. I screamed and looked down. It was a carrier bag containing all our goodies. Mum and Dad must have put it there. They are truly the best!

"Hey guys, I'm back!" I called.

I emptied the bag on to my bed and we all snuggled up together and dipped in. There were jelly babies and Love Hearts, fruit salads, three Kit-Kats, a tube of Smarties and a huge packet of popcorn. Kenny kept flicking the popcorn at the rest of us and then somehow we all joined in. Popcorn and sweets flew around my room like an alien snowstorm.

Suddenly, I heard a familiar squeak on the stairs. My parents must be coming to bed and they were bound to check up on us.

"Quick! My parents!" I hissed.

We all scrambled inside our sleeping bags and turned off our torches. Sure enough, the door opened and a chink of light spilt across the floor. I prayed that whoever was looking in wouldn't see all the mess of food around the beds. They mustn't have done, because the door closed and nothing was said.

"I love a good food fight!" Kenny whispered when they had gone. We all agreed.

"We could have one in the open air tomorrow. That's even better!" said Lyndz excitedly.

Somewhere, deep inside my brain, the cogs began to turn. I could feel an idea forming.

"That's it!" I shouted. "I've got it! We could have a food fight and bombard the M&Ms. If we get to the park early enough we'll be there before them. So *we'll* have the advantage."

"Frankie *brain-box* Thomas strikes again!" laughed Kenny. "That's a brilliant idea. I know the perfect place where we can see the park gates but where we'll be hidden from view."

"We can make lots of jellies and stuff," said Rosie.

"And my parents won't know. They'll just think it's for the picnic." I laughed. I must admit, sometimes I even surprise myself with my outstanding brain power!

We all chatted about the kind of foods we needed and how best to humiliate the M&Ms. Suddenly there was a banging on my door.

"Come on girls! It's after one o'clock," shouted my dad. "Some of us need our beauty sleep, you know. If you don't go to sleep now, you'll be too tired for your picnic tomorrow!"

The last thing I heard before closing my eyes was Kenny talking in her sleep.

"Jelly tutus. Popcorn knickers. Splat!"

She's crazy, that friend of mine.

# CHAPTER EIGHT

The next morning I woke up really early. It was partly because I was so excited, partly because the sun was streaming through my curtains. And partly because two noisy blackbirds had decided to perform an opera outside my bedroom window.

"Shoot them Frankie, please!" said a muffled voice. It was Kenny. She had her head buried beneath her pillow.

I looked at my watch. It was only 5.30 am which was kind of early to be getting up. I peeped over the top of my sleeping bag. Rosie was tossing and turning and looking very restless, which meant that she was about to wake up. I couldn't really see much of Fliss on the top bunk-bed, but she seemed to be asleep. Then the whistling started. It was loud. It was tuneless. It was Lyndz!

"Shut up!" yelled Kenny. Her head was still under her pillow.

"I've been listening to those birds for hours," said Lyndz in between whistles. "And I don't see why I should be the only one awake!"

"That's just selfish," grumbled Fliss. She's always like a bear with a sore head first thing in the morning.

"Well, now we're all awake, what shall we do?" asked Lyndz, sitting up in her sleeping bag. I don't know how she manages it, but Lyndz always seems to be full of beans. The rest of us can get really ratty, as you probably know by now. But Lyndz always seems to be bright and cheerful. Not that I felt like being bright and cheerful with her at half-past five in the morning!

"Come on, Lyndz, give us a break," I said. "We can't do anything much because we'll wake my parents. And they would *not* be pleased."

"We don't have to do anything noisy," Lyndz pleaded.

Lyndz doing something quietly was about as likely as Mr Blobby joining Boyzone.

"Er, like when are you ever quiet?" asked Kenny, who had now emerged from under her pillow. Kenny is *not* a morning person!

"I can be quiet," argued Lyndz. "It's just that in my house, if you're not loud, you don't get heard."

That was true. With four brothers to compete with, Lyndz had to make a lot of noise.

"Couldn't we have a round of International Gladiators?" pleaded Lyndz. "We can play it quietly."

Who was she trying to kid? When we play any Gladiator games, my dad says we sound like screaming banshees, whatever they are.

"Besides," argued Lyndz. "We could probably do with the practice."

"What do you mean?" I asked. It wasn't as though we were going to compete against anybody else. We only do it for fun.

"We need to get our throwing arms warmed up for our food fight!" Lyndz laughed, triumphantly.

As soon as she'd said that, Kenny sat bolt upright. It was as though someone had just wound her up.

"Lyndz's right," she yelled. "We do need to practise. I can't believe that I'd actually forgotten about the M&Ms!"

"Sshhh!" I whispered. "You're going to wake Mum and Dad and that's the last thing I need. If they find out what we've got planned, I'm dead!"

"We could just practise throwing soft things," said Kenny, lobbing a sock at Fliss.

"Get off!" grumbled Fliss from her sleeping bag. "We don't need to practise throwing things. We're all in the netball team, aren't we?"

"I'm not," said Rosie.

"Yes, but you should be," said Lyndz and I quickly. Rosie not being in the netball team was a bit of a sore point all round. She plays Centre, the same as Fliss, so they can't both be in the team at the same time.

"Anyway," I tried to reason with Kenny, "surely we can all throw jellies and stuff. It can't be so difficult."

"Oh no!" shouted Rosie suddenly. "Jellies! We should have made them last night. They'll never set in time."

She was right of course. Although I didn't

think Mum and Dad would have been too pleased if we'd been in the kitchen at one in the morning. "Look, it only needs two of us to make the jellies," I said, taking charge. "So I'll go with Rosie and the rest of you can stay here."

We crept downstairs and into the kitchen. I found a few packets of jelly in one of the cupboards.

"Can you imagine what disasters we would have had if Kenny and Lyndz had been helping?" I said. We both laughed.

I know that I wasn't sure about Rosie when she joined the Sleepover Club at first. But it's kind of nice having another sensible person in the group.

We very carefully put the bowls of jelly into the fridge. One of the ones I was carrying slopped over the bowl a bit. I wiped up the mess then threw all the empty jelly packets away. Mum and Dad would never know we'd been in the kitchen.

"We'd better see what chaos the others are causing," I said to Rosie.

As soon as I got half-way up the stairs, I heard the screaming. And I knew that I was in trouble.

Rosie and I ran up to my room. But Dad had beaten us to it. His face was like thunder.

"Right, young lady," he said angrily to me. "Just what do you think you're playing at?"

"We just went downstairs to make you and Mrs Thomas a cup of tea," lied Rosie, very calmly. "But then we realised how early it was and thought that you might not be awake yet."

"Well, as you can see, Rosie, I am awake," said Dad. His eyes looked very sleepy behind his glasses. "And I wonder just why I am awake so early on a Sunday morning." Screams and shouts were still echoing from inside my room. Dad threw open the door. None of us was prepared for the scene which met us.

The floor was already covered in popcorn and sweet wrappers from the night before. Now it was also littered with socks and knickers and Lyndz. She was sort of stuck underneath the camp-bed. Kenny was tickling her feet, which Lyndz absolutely hates. Fliss was still in bed, but was throwing things at Kenny. As we stood in the doorway her furry orange octopus came hurtling towards us. It hit Dad right in the face and knocked his glasses to the floor.

As soon as she saw what she'd done, Fliss screamed and got out of bed. Unfortunately she forgot that she was in the top bunk. She fell to the floor with a loud thud.

Rosie and I rushed over to her.

"Are you all right?" we gasped. This sleepover was fast turning into an episode of *Casualty*.

"Yes, I think so," Fliss whimpered. She got up slowly and rubbed her back.

"I think it's just shock," he said gently. "What about making that tea, Rosie? And as for the rest of you—" Dad looked sternly at Kenny, Lyndz and me. "Do you always behave like gorillas at this time in the morning?"

"But Dad, I wasn't even here!" I protested.

"That's no excuse," he said. "Your friends are your guests. And it's up to you to make sure that *they* behave as we expect *you* to."

"Sorry, Mr Thomas," muttered Kenny and Lyndz. They were both blushing furiously. It's always so much worse being told off by someone else's father, isn't it?

"If I was a really awful father I wouldn't let you go on your picnic," Dad said.

We all protested. Very loudly.

"But as I'm a very nice man, you can still go

IF you promise to be good – AND CLEAN UP THIS MESS! But I'm warning you – one more incident like this and you're never going out again."

We started to scramble about on the floor, scooping popcorn into our hands. Rosie appeared with a tray of tea. One cup was for Fliss and one each for Mum and Dad. She really is very thoughtful.

We were on our best behaviour for the rest of the morning.

"You really should have asked permission," said Mum, putting the jelly back in the fridge.

"I know, but we completely forgot about them and we wanted them to be set for the picnic," I explained.

"I'm not sure that they will be, love," said Mum. "You might have to forget about them."

"We can take them anyway. It's cool to *drink* jelly at the moment," said Rosie quickly.

"Not much good for throwing though," grumbled Kenny. I shot her one of my looks. She was getting as bad as Fliss.

"I hope you're not going to do anything silly," warned Dad sternly. "I don't want to have to bail you all out from the police station for causing trouble in the park." The five of us exchanged looks.

"As if!" I exclaimed, looking very hurt. "We're going to have a nice civilised picnic." I hate lying to Mum and Dad.

"Well I'm very pleased to hear it!" laughed Mum. "Now Fliss, where is this concert that Callum's in? I thought we might go along to watch and catch up with your Mum and Andy."

"Is Callum any good?" asked Rosie.

"No, he's useless!" laughed Fliss. "He keeps tripping up! Flora's supposed to be good, though. Mum says her teacher thinks she could be famous one day!"

"Is Flora Callum's girlfriend?" I asked. "The one we saw him with at the fair?"

"Yep. Apparently she's so good, some of the older girls are jealous of her. I think they can be quite mean, too. Anyway, she's got Callum to protect her now! He's like a limpet – he's always right by her side."

"Even when she goes to the toilet? Yuk!" exclaimed Kenny, and we all laughed.

# CHAPTER NINE

We spent the rest of the morning getting ready for our picnic. Kenny kept on her grubby Leicester City football shirt; the rest of us put on shorts and cropped tops. We fluffed our hair up a bit and put Body Shop fruity lip balm on our lips. As I was rummaging about in my drawer for a sparkly bangle, I found some *Silly String* which was left over from Christmas.

"Coo-el!" said Kenny when she saw it. "That's just what we need for spraying at the M&Ms."

"Yeah, it'll get stuck in their hair, and they'll hate that!" laughed Rosie.

"Right, you lot!" Mum called upstairs. "If you get your picnic food ready quickly, we'll give you a lift to the park. I know that it's near enough to walk there, but we'll be passing it anyway. We're going round to your house, Fliss to find out from your mum where this concert is."

Poor Dad! I knew this wasn't exactly his idea of fun.

As we piled into the car, we were all pretty hyped up. Mum and Dad exchanged glances. They know how silly we can get.

When we got to the park, Dad pulled over.

"Right, you lot," he said very seriously. "I'll pick you up by the park gates at four. Don't be late. Have a good time and don't get too silly."

"Chill out, Dad!" I said. "We'll be as good as gold!" Kenny started to giggle.

"Yes, fool's gold!" said Dad and drove off.

We all skipped into the park, singing *Wannabe* at the tops of our voices.

The park was kind of busy. Busier than we had expected. We panicked a bit that we wouldn't be able to find a good spot for the food fight. The secluded place that Kenny knew was already taken. We had just assumed that it would be free. A young couple was already there, having a romantic picnic.

"What are we going to do now?" hissed Rosie. "We can't have a food fight if *they're* here."

"Maybe we should just go somewhere else and forget about the M&Ms," whispered Fliss nervously.

"No, we're staying," said Kenny firmly. "Let's unpack the picnic."

We spread out a rug and began to unpack all our boxes of food. Kenny suddenly began to behave like a chimpanzee. She started grunting and bent over so that her knuckles were scraping the ground. Then she began to screech and pretended to pick fleas off her arms. I know that she can be strange sometimes but I'd never seen her doing anything like that before. The rest of us stared at her, and so did the young couple. After a few minutes of tutting and sighing, they packed up their things and moved away.

"I knew that would work!" laughed Kenny triumphantly.

I felt a bit guilty, but I was relieved that we were by ourselves. When anybody else poked their head around the corner, Kenny did her chimpanzee act and they soon cleared off again.

I don't know about you, but I always plan everything very clearly in my head. I always know exactly what I'm going to do in certain situations. Then, when it becomes reality, I just freeze up. I guess I'm always braver in my thoughts. That's exactly what happened that day with our food fight. I was so brave talking about it beforehand, but when we were actually in the park I started to get butterflies. I didn't want to be there at all.

I don't think that I was the only one who felt like that either, because none of us spoke to each other. Fliss, Lyndz, Rosie and I just stared at all the food we had brought for the picnic. We couldn't face eating anything. Kenny could. She's much braver than the rest of us. I just sat there with a sick feeling in my stomach. Fliss had been right. We should have gone somewhere else and left the M&Ms alone.

We took it in turns to keep watch on the gates through a small hole in the hedge. Half an hour passed and there was still no sign of Emma Hughes and Emily Berryman.

"Maybe we got the wrong end of the stick," said Rosie. "Maybe the M&Ms aren't coming to the park at all."

I hoped that she was right. I don't like being

wrong usually, but I wouldn't have minded being wrong about this.

I took my turn at keeping watch. There seemed to be lots of young girls, about six years old, all dressed up in frilly dresses. I thought it must be someone's birthday and they were going to have their party in the park. I wished that I was that age again. Life didn't seem so complicated when I was six.

Then I thought that I saw Fliss's mum with her partner, Andy. And I was sure that I saw Callum with them. And Flora.

"Hey Fliss, I thought Callum was supposed to be in a concert this afternoon," I called.

"He is. Why?" she asked.

"Because I've just seen him with your mum and Andy."

"WHAT?" Fliss yelled. She pushed me out of the way so that she could get a clear look herself. "What on earth are they doing *here*?" she said in a kind of strangled voice. Then she screamed.

"They're not the only people either," she yelled. "The M&Ms are here. And they're coming this way!"

# CHAPTER TEN

We all crowded round Fliss and strained to peep through the hedge. The M&Ms were standing right in front of us on the other side.

"That's what I saw them wearing yesterday," whispered Rosie. Emma Hughes and Emily Berryman were wearing frilly tutus of the palest pink. Tight blonde buns sat on the tops of their heads. Not a hair was out of place. Emily Berryman suddenly turned towards us. We all crouched down and held our breath. If she saw us now, we were dead. But she was only asking Emma Hughes to check that her bun was secure.

"Get a life!" muttered Kenny.

"Ssh!" I hissed.

The M&Ms couldn't have heard because they turned away from us and started doing little pirouettes across the grass.

"What do they look like!" snorted Lyndz, trying to keep as quiet as possible.

"Show-offs!" muttered Kenny. She grabbed a handful of jelly.

"Wait!" I shouted. "Let's get organised first."

"Maybe we should pack away the stuff we're not going to use," suggested Rosie. "You know, just in case we have to make a quick exit."

"Good thinking, Batman," I said.

We shoved uneaten sandwiches and biscuits back into plastic bags. Then we put the jelly, *Silly String* and a few squelchy sandwiches in front of the hedge. Rosie put five plastic spoons in the jelly so that we could use them as catapults.

Whilst we were preparing ourselves, there seemed to be an increasing amount of noise on the other side of the hedge. The sound of chattering and giggling floated over to us. Rosie went to have a look to see where all the noise was coming from.

"It's only the little girls in their party dresses. Some of them look kind of familiar, I don't know why," she said, looking puzzled. "The M&Ms don't look very happy anyway. I don't know why they're even standing so close to them. We all know that they don't like being associated with *babies*, don't we!" We all laughed.

Just at that moment some screechy music began to play. It was horrible, but I was sure that I'd heard it somewhere before.

Kenny pushed Rosie out of the way and had a look through a gap in the hedge.

"All I can see is the M&Ms dancing and making prats of themselves," she snorted. "The other girls are just gawping at them. Come on, let's get the M & Ms!" We all bent down and picked up our ammunition.

"Right," shouted Kenny. "FIRE!"

Rosie and Fliss grabbed the cans of *Silly String* and sprayed them through the gap in the hedge. The rest of us grabbed spoonfuls of jelly and tried to catapult them over to the other side. There was a bit of a knack to getting the spoon at just the right angle. At first, as much jelly slopped down over us as it did over the hedge. But soon we got into the swing of it and there was no stopping us.

Jelly flew everywhere. It was impossible to look through the hedge and throw at the same time, so we just kept throwing. We knew that some of the jelly was hitting the target, because we heard the M&Ms shrieking. Well, we *assumed* it was the M&Ms. Lyndz and Kenny were giggling so much, it was hard to tell.

I was covered in jelly. We all were. Fliss had emptied her can of *Silly String* and had now moved on to throwing jelly. Considering that she hadn't wanted to have the food fight at all, she was enjoying herself as much as anybody.

When Rosie had finished spraying her *Silly String* she crept to the edge of the hedge and peeped round the corner to see what was happening on the other side.

It's funny because from that moment, everything seemed to go into slow motion. When Rosie turned back towards us she was very red in the face. She started to wave her arms about as though she was a fly who'd just been zapped by fly spray. We all stopped firing our jelly. All except Fliss who was having the time of her life.

Something inside my brain clicked, too. And I realised that the music, which was still going, was the music that the M&Ms had been dancing to in the studio at school. Not that we could hear much of the music any more because the air was suddenly filled with angry voices and children crying.

We all crowded round the gap in the hedge and peeped through. The scene on the other side looked like a battlefield. Small girls were on the ground in tears. Their dresses were covered in jelly stains and *Silly String* festooned their hair. The grass glistened with a jelly cover, and skid marks cut across it. You could trace where the girls had fallen. Adults were clustering round them and lots of angry faces were turned towards the hedge.

We knew that we had to get out of there as quickly as possible. But we couldn't help taking a moment to savour the state of the M&Ms. They were slumped on the grass. *Silly String* clung to their clothes and their hair like cobwebs. Their tutus weren't pale pink any more, but streaky purple and red, with grass and mud stains up the back.

Fliss was oblivious to the chaos and was happily continuing to fire jelly. She took aim and – SPLODGE! – the jelly landed right on one poor boy's head. On closer inspection the boy turned out to be Callum in his ballet tights. Andy was with him and – no, it couldn't be! Yes, it was – my mum! Not only that, but we could see Fliss's mum marching towards us. It was time to leave. And fast!

"Fliss. Come on! Your mum's heading this way!" I yelled, throwing some carrier bags at her.

That was enough to stop Fliss in her tracks.

"How do you know?"

"We've just seen her," I tried to stay calm. "My mum's here, too. Looking after *your* brother, who you've just hit with jelly!"

"Oh no! His concert must have been here. And that's why the M&Ms were here. I think they go to the same dancing school."

I wanted to smack Fliss and find out why she hadn't given us that little nugget of information sooner, but Kenny shouted, "Don't go out of the main gate! Everybody'll see us. I know a way out through the fence. Come on. Hurry up!"

We all started running. Legs and arms were everywhere as we tried to cope with all the carrier bags full of picnic things. They seemed to get heavier with every step.

I looked round as I ran to see if we were being followed. I could see Fliss's mum in the distance, and a few more angry parents. I could also hear the park's security guard shouting that we were banned from the park for life! A hand suddenly grabbed me and yanked me into the bushes. I screamed but a voice said, "Shut up!"

It was Kenny. She had found the way out of the park and she thought I was going to run past it. Boy was I glad to see the other side of the fence.

We carried on running though, until we were well out of sight of the park. Then we dropped our bags on to the pavement and collapsed in a heap.

When I had got my breath back, I asked Fliss what she had meant about the M&Ms being in the same concert as Callum and Flora.

"I think they must be the girls who have been so horrid to Flora because she got better marks in her exam than they did," admitted Fliss sheepishly.

"And you couldn't have told us this before?" I asked crossly.

"Well, I did say there was something worrying me about this whole thing, didn't I?" Fliss snapped back. "I just couldn't remember what it was."

"You mean, the babies they were talking about weren't us, but those other little girls in the concert?" asked Lyndz. "It must have been *them* who the M&Ms had seen with their parents at the fair."

"And it must have been *Flora* who they

thought acted like a goddess, not *Laura*!" said Rosie.

I thought that Kenny was going to be furious with Fliss about the whole mix-up, but she couldn't stop smiling.

"It was worth it just to see those stupid M&Ms in such a mess!" she kept saying.

"Hey, what are we going to do about your dad?" Rosie suddenly asked me. "He's supposed to be picking us up by the park gates at four."

"Rats! I hadn't thought of that!" I said.

"Oh, but I had!" said a man's voice behind us.

It was Dad.

Well, that all happened about a month ago. We haven't been allowed to have any sleepovers since, but that's no surprise. We did see each other at school until we broke up for summer, and at Brownies.

We were all grounded but things have relaxed a bit now and I've seen Kenny, Lyndz and Rosie a few times. We've been to each others' houses to play records and stuff but we haven't seen much of Fliss. She hasn't been allowed to hang out with the rest of us at all. Her mum thinks that we are a bad influence on her precious daughter. When she picked Fliss up from Brownies, she wouldn't even *look* at the rest of us. All I can say is that she obviously hadn't seen her daughter throwing that jelly. Fliss was like a different person! It was weird!

As far as the M&Ms are concerned, they know that it was us who ruined their concert, but they haven't taken their revenge – yet! It was strange, because when they saw us at school the next day, they didn't say anything. Nothing at all! It was the first time we could ever remember them *not* having a dig at us. Kenny reckons they were just too embarrassed. And of course she's thrilled that we finally gained a victory over them. It's the summer holidays now and there's no more Brownies for a while so we haven't really seen the M&Ms much. They're bound to have something planned for us though, so we're keeping our ears open.

Here we are at Fliss's. Let's go and see if her mum will let her come out. And remember – not a word about parks and flying jelly!

# The Sleepover Club
# Sleeps Out

# CHAPTER ONE

Hiya! It's me.

No, just for once this isn't Frankie. Bet that's given you a bit of a shock, hasn't it?

No, I'm not Fliss either. P-lease!

And I'm not Rosie. Guess again.

Wrong! It's not Lyndz.

It's me.

Kenny! Or, if you want to annoy me seriously, you can call me Laura. No-one calls me Laura except my mum when she's in a mood. If you want us to be mates, you'll never, ever let the L-word cross your lips.

I guess that by now you've realised that

9

you're stuck with me, instead of Frankie. Hey, you don't have to look so shocked. I don't know what Frankie's told you about me, but it's all lies. I'm not wild at all. I'm perfectly house-trained (joke). Well, most of the time, anyway.

The point is, Frankie's told you everything about the Sleepover Club up till now, and why should she have all the fun? I told her it was about time one of the rest of us got to talk to you for a change, and Frankie was cool about it. She's cool about most things. That's why she's my best mate. (I had to bribe her with a bag of Wotsits, but that's another story).

I wasn't the only one who wanted to tell you about the sleepover last Friday night. Once we'd decided that someone else instead of Frankie was going to do it, Fliss and Rosie and Lyndz were all dying to get in on the act, too. That's because our last sleepover was brilliant, one of the best ever. We had a totally radical time, and best of all, we completely trashed the M&Ms. Anyway, we argued for half-an-hour over who was going to tell you about it, and then Frankie persuaded the others that it ought to be me. That wasn't just because I gave her my Wotsits, but because it was me the M&Ms did the dirty on, and getting revenge was my idea.

Whoops, hang on a sec. I'm getting ahead of myself. I'm not as good at this as Frankie. I need a bit more practice. Hmm. D'you know what? I reckon the beginning would be a really excellent place to start.

You know all about the Sleepover Club, don't you? There's just the five of us – Frankie, Fliss, Lyndz, Rosie and me, and we sleep over at each other's houses every week-end. OK, OK, so you know all that. Don't get your intestines in a twist. I just thought that maybe if you hadn't been around before, you might not know. That's all. (You know what intestines are, don't you? They're these sort of tubes inside your stomach. I want to be a doctor, so I know about things like that. The others think I'm completely gross.)

Maybe I ought to remind you about the M&Ms as well. Remember them? Emma

Hughes and Emily Berryman? The Queen and The Goblin? The Gruesome Twosome? They're in our class at school, and they are the biggest enemies of the Sleepover Club in the whole world. If it hadn't been for the M&Ms playing that horrible trick on me, I'd never have come up with such a brilliant plan to get our own back.

Sorry, I'm doing it again. My mouth's got a mind of its own. My sister Monster-Features (my parents named her Molly, but Monster-Features sounds so-o-o much better) says if my brain was as big as my mouth, I'd be a genius, but what does she know? I never talk to her, except to fight. Yesterday I wanted to phone Frankie to talk about the sleepover, and Molly the Monster wanted to phone some stoo-pid friend of hers, and we got into a humungous argument, and I picked up the Yellow Pages and – but that's another story.

Come on, let's go, and I'll tell you what happened. And this time I'll start right at the very beginning.

# CHAPTER TWO

It all started last week, on a really wet, cold and miserable day. We'd got soaked to the skin walking to school, and the only good thing was that it was a Friday. And that night we were all sleeping over at Frankie's.

"I asked my mum if we could make popcorn tonight," Frankie said as we went into the classroom.

"Really?" Fliss, who was fussing with her wet hair, looked impressed. The Sleepover Club have been banned from every kitchen in the universe since we nearly burnt her mum's house down. "What did she say?"

13

Frankie grinned. "She said over her dead body."

"Well, what are we going to do tonight then?" Fliss persisted. You must have sussed out by now that Fliss is just a tiny bit of a fusspot. "We could have a hair-styling contest."

"No, let's have a disco," Rosie chimed in. "I've got my new Spice Girls tape."

"Why don't we play Twister?" Lyndz suggested.

I opened my mouth to say I wanted to tell horror stories (I always want to tell horror stories at Sleepovers, but we hardly ever do, because Fliss is a bit of a wimp and gets scared), when suddenly I noticed the M&Ms coming towards us with their ears flapping.

"Hold on a minute, girls," I said, pretending to sniff the air. "There's a horrible smell around here."

The others clocked the M&Ms, and started to giggle.

"Oh, very funny," said Emma Hughes snootily. We call her the Queen because she

14

thinks she *is* one. She goes around with her nose stuck in the air like the rest of us stink or something. If she ever went to Buckingham Palace, she'd expect the real Queen to curtsey to her. What's really irritating, though, is that all the teachers think she's wonderful.

"As if we wanted to listen to what idiots like you were saying anyway," growled Emily Berryman (The Goblin). We call her that because she's really tiny with great big eyes and a deep voice. If you put a hat on her and gave her a fishing rod, she'd look exactly like a garden gnome.

"Oh, yeah?" I said. "Well, your ears were flapping so much, you looked like you were about to take off and fly round the classroom."

"Like Dumbo," Frankie added, and we all fell about.

Emma turned red with anger. She likes to think she's perfect, but the truth is, her ears do stick out just a little bit. She opened her mouth to say something nasty in return, but just then Mrs Weaver, our teacher, came in with the register under her arm.

"Sit down, everyone," she said, looking round.

The M&Ms skipped smartly off to their table on the other side of the classroom, and I rolled my eyes at Frankie. It's s-o-o-o annoying the way the Gruesome Twosome smarm up to the teachers, and pretend to be all sweet and nice, when really they're stuck-up nerds.

Mrs Weaver sat down at her desk, and everyone stopped fidgeting and shut up. Mrs Weaver's OK, but it's best not to push her too far. Know what I mean?

"Before I do the register, I want to talk to you about our end-of-term trip next Friday." Mrs Weaver beamed round at us as if she was planning to take the whole class to EuroDisney. "We'll be going to visit the Armfield Museum, near Leicester, next Friday afternoon."

"Oh, great big fat hairy deal," I mouthed at the others. We've been to the Armfield Museum with the school a zillion times, plus our parents are always taking us there when it rains in the holidays, and there's nothing else to do. We've been there so many times, it's about as exciting as cutting your toenails. The rest of the class looked just as unimpressed as we did, and everyone started muttering and moaning under their breath.

"Awesome! The Armfield Museum!" Frankie said, just a bit sarcastically. "I'm s-o-o-o glad we're not going to Alton Towers or some other boring old theme park where we might have some fun."

"Oh, me too!" I joined in. "Who wants to go on a pathetic log flume when they could be looking at a load of broken old pots?"

Rosie was looking a bit blank.

"What's the Armfield Museum?" she asked. Rosie's fitted in so well into the Sleepover Club, that we keep forgetting she hasn't been here that long.

"Funnily enough, it's a museum," I grinned.

"It's OK, really," said Lyndz. "It's got loads of spooky stuff like Egyptian mummies."

"Yeah, but when you've seen one mummy,

you've seen them all," said Fliss gloomily, and she looked so depressed, the rest of us started to giggle.

"When you've quite finished," said Mrs Weaver, glaring round at everyone. The whole class shut up and looked at her again.

"This trip to the museum will be very different from other visits," Mrs Weaver went on. "We'll be having a guided tour, and workshop activities, but we will also be taking sleeping bags and sleeping overnight in the museum galleries."

Well, that did it. The whole class went bananas, including the Sleepover Club.

"Awesome!" Frankie said again, but this time she meant it. "A sleepover in a museum!"

"The Sleepover Club sleeps out!" Lyndz said. "Excellent!"

"D'you think they'll let us sleep in the room with the Egyptian mummies in it?" I asked eagerly. Then I clocked Fliss, who was looking a bit pea-green. "What's biting you, Flissy?"

Fliss was looking as if she was going to be sick.

"I don't think I want to sleep over in a museum," she mumbled. "It'll be scary."

"You bet it will," I said. "That's why it'll be excellent."

Fliss looked even more spooked, and Frankie stuck her elbow in my ribs.

"Ow! What I mean is, it won't be scary, Fliss. Not really. We'll all be there to look after you."

"Anyway, you can hold hands with Ryan Scott if you get scared, Fliss," Lyndz said wickedly.

Fliss turned pink. We think boys are mostly pretty r-e-e-e-volting, but Fliss has a bit of a thing about Ryan Scott, who's in our class.

"Ssshh!" Fliss whispered, glancing round at Ryan who sat at the table behind us. "He might hear you!"

"I never thought we'd be going to a sleepover with boys," I said, which started us all giggling.

"Or teachers," Rosie pointed out.

"Or the M&Ms," Lyndz said.

That stopped us laughing. We all looked across the classroom at the Gruesome

Twosome, who saw us staring, and stuck their noses in the air. I put my hands behind my ears, and waggled them at Emma, who turned purple with rage.

"We won't have to sleep in the same room as them, will we?" Rosie asked anxiously.

"I'd rather sleep with the Egyptian mummies," said Fliss. She was deadly serious too, which set us all off again.

Mrs Weaver had been trying to get us quiet again for the last five minutes, and now she'd just about managed it.

"I've got some letters for your parents with more details about the trip, which I'll give out tonight." Some people were still fidgeting with excitement and whispering to each other, and Mrs W glared at them until they stopped.

"And now it's time to settle down and get on with some work. Blue and Green groups – Maths, Yellow and Red groups – topic workbooks. Oh, and Kenny—"

I jumped. I'd been daydreaming about Armfield Museum and wondering if I'd get a chance to shut the M&Ms inside one of those big mummy cases.

"Yes, Mrs Weaver?"

"It's your turn to use the computer." Mrs Weaver had to raise her voice because everyone else was already moving round, collecting their work from their lockers. "You'd better get on with that story you started last week."

"OK, Miss." I was well pleased. I love using the computer. The only thing is, it's over the other side of the classroom, right next to the M&Ms' table.

"Hey, Emily," Emma said as I walked past them to get to the computer, "have you noticed that there's a really horrible smell around here?"

"Oh, p-*lease*!" I said, sitting down at the computer desk. "I think I've heard that one before. You two have got no imagination!"

The M&Ms both turned red.

"You think you're so clever, don't you!" Emma spluttered.

I grinned at her.

"By the way, Mrs Weaver's watching you

two," I said under my breath.

The M&Ms both jumped, looked scared and quickly opened their maths books. I nearly died laughing. Mrs Weaver was actually writing on the blackboard, and had her back to the class.

"One up to me!" I said, and I licked my finger and drew a '1' in the air. Then I turned my back on the Gruesome Twosome, and switched the computer on. I could hear them muttering to each other behind me, but I ignored them.

I found my work, and read through what I'd already written. It was a really ace story about the Loch Ness monster, and I was looking forward to finishing it and reading it at the sleepover tonight. It was so bloodthirsty, it would probably frighten Fliss into fits!

After a quarter-of-an-hour, though, I'd only written three words. Three words! At this rate I wouldn't finish the story till next Christmas. The trouble was, it was impossible to concentrate. Everyone was supposed to be working quietly, but they were so excited about the museum sleepover, that they just couldn't stop talking about it. However hard Mrs Weaver tried, she couldn't shut the class up. To make things worse, one of the maths groups was measuring all the furniture in the classroom, and they kept accidentally whacking each other with the metre sticks, like actors in a silent movie.

Like I said, it was impossible to concentrate. But I can always concentrate better when I'm using the computer if I'm eating at the same time. That was when I remembered the Opal Fruits in my jacket in the cloakroom. There were a couple of lime-green ones in there with my name on them! My mouth began to water.

I looked round. Mrs Weaver had disappeared into the book cupboard, and Ryan Scott and his sidekick Danny McCloud were fighting a duel with their metre sticks. No-one would notice if I just ducked out for a moment, and got my sweets. No, of course we aren't supposed to leave the classroom without permission, but then we're not supposed to eat sweets in class either!

"Where're you going?" Fliss asked as I sprinted over to the classroom door. That girl's got eyes in the back of her head, I swear.

"To get my Opal Fruits," I muttered, one eye fixed firmly on the book cupboard.

"Have you asked Mrs Weaver?" Fliss said sternly.

"Oh, sure," I said, "like I really want a detention that much."

"But, Kenny—" Fliss began, looking shocked. I ignored her. I was out, and back inside the classroom with my Opal Fruits hidden up my sleeve in one minute flat. Fliss looked outraged, but I winked at the others, who started laughing. Mrs Weaver had come out of the book cupboard, but she was busy examining Danny McCloud's eye where Ryan Scott had poked him with the metre stick, so she didn't notice me. I hurried back to the computer, and sat down. And that was when I got a BIG shock.

The first thing I saw was that my story had gone. Vanished. In its place was just one sentence. A single sentence repeated over and over again, from the top of the computer screen right down to the bottom.

*Mrs Weaver stinks.*

My jaw hit the floor. I was so shocked, I sat there staring at the computer screen, wondering what had happened. Then I realised in a flash – the M&Ms! Those nasty little nerds had done this. I just hoped I could get my story back, but first I had to get rid of the stuff on-screen before anyone saw it. I reached for the mouse, but I was already too late. I heard a voice behind me.

"How are you getting on, Kenny?"

It was Mrs Weaver. She looked at the screen, and then looked again as if she couldn't believe her eyes.

There was silence for a few moments. Somehow the rest of the class picked up that something was going on, and gradually they went quiet too, until there was a horrible silence in the whole of the room. And during that silence, the words on the screen seemed to be growing, getting bigger and bigger and blacker and blacker.

"Well, I'm surprised at you, Laura," Mrs Weaver said at last, and I could tell from her voice how annoyed she was. She didn't usually call me Laura, but this time I wasn't about to argue. "If that's how you want to waste your time, then you'd better make up for it in detention today. Now clear that rubbish off the screen, and get back to your table."

"But, Miss, I didn't write that," I began, and then I stopped. I couldn't say that the M&Ms had set me up while I went out of class (without permission) to get sweets I wasn't supposed to be eating, could I? I'd still be in trouble, whatever.

Mrs Weaver just looked at me, and walked off. I deleted all the writing, and switched the computer off. Behind me the M&Ms were giggling and nudging each other, but I ignored them, and went back to my table.

The rest of the Sleepover Club looked as shocked as I felt. Fliss was nearly crying, and Frankie, Rosie and Lyndz were as white as ghosts. As for me, I was so angry, I was boiling. I could have gone right back across the classroom, grabbed Emma Hughes and shaken her until she owned up.

"It was the M&Ms, right?" Frankie whispered in my ear as I sat down next to her. "What did they do?"

"Deleted my story, and wrote *Mrs Weaver stinks*. A zillion times." I glanced across the classroom at the M&Ms. They were smirking, and patting each other on the back. Emma saw me looking, and she licked her finger and drew a '1' in the air. I clenched my fists.

"Keep cool, Kenny," Frankie said anxiously. "Don't let her get to you."

"The rotten pigs!" said Lyndz. "We're not going to let them get away with that, are we?"

I shook my head. "No way," I muttered. "It's about time the M&Ms learned that they can't mess the Sleepover Club around."

# CHAPTER THREE

"Look, we've got to decide what we're going to do," Frankie said, for about the zillionth time. "If we don't get our own back, the M&Ms'll never let us forget it."

We all nodded, but none of us said anything. We were too depressed. We were sitting in Frankie's back garden, the sun had started shining and we were eating pizza, but we were still miserable. That was because we couldn't believe the nerve of the M&Ms.

"I still can't believe they did it," Lyndz said. "I mean, the M&Ms are so goody-goody and all that."

"Yeah, I would've thought they'd be

scared of getting caught," Rosie agreed.

"Well, there wasn't much chance of that, was there?" Frankie pointed out. "Mrs Weaver was in the book cupboard, and everyone else was watching Ryan and Danny fighting with the metre sticks."

"And Emma was so close to the computer, she wouldn't even have had to get out of her chair," I said. "You know what I was really worried about? I thought Mrs Weaver might say I couldn't come to the museum sleepover."

"Yeah, you were lucky to get away with just a detention," agreed Frankie.

We all sat gloomily looking down at our pizzas. Not even the thought of the museum sleepover could cheer us up at the moment.

"You should have told Mrs Weaver it wasn't you, Kenny," Fliss said, also for the zillionth time.

"I did, and she didn't believe me," I said impatiently.

"You could have told her it was the

M&Ms," Fliss persisted. That girl never knows when to give up. I glared at her.

"I'm not a snitcher!"

"Anyway, Mrs Weaver wouldn't have believed you," Frankie cut in quickly. Just in time to stop me throwing a half-eaten slice of pizza at Fliss.

After what had happened, I wouldn't have got through the rest of the day if it hadn't been for the others. The M&Ms were real pigs. They kept staring at me and giggling, and looking really smug and pleased with themselves, and they made me so angry, I could have gone over there and knocked their heads together. I think Frankie and the others were a bit worried I might actually do it, because they'd stuck to my side like glue all day.

"Come on, someone must have a really good idea for getting our revenge on the M&Ms," Frankie said. "We've got to think of something."

"What have Emily and Emma done now?" Frankie's mum asked, coming towards us with a jug of lemonade. No-one had even noticed her come out of the house, and I wondered how much she'd overheard.

"Nothing!" we all said together. Well, all of us except Fliss.

"They played this really horrible trick on Kenny," she said breathlessly. "What they did was, they – OW!"

Fliss was sitting between Frankie and Lyndz, so one of them must have kicked her leg. Quite hard, too, from the look on Fliss's face. She turned pink, and shut up. I like Frankie's mum a lot, but this wasn't something we wanted to tell grown-ups about. This was private, Sleepover Club business.

Frankie's mum raised her eyebrows and waited, but we all just looked innocently at her. We're good at that. Well, Fliss goes bright red after about ten seconds, but the rest of us are brilliant at it.

I don't think Mrs Thomas was fooled, though. But she didn't say anything except, "Who wants some lemonade?" She filled our glasses, and then went back into the house.

"Who kicked me?" Fliss demanded crossly.

"Not me," Frankie said innocently.

"Nor me," said Lyndz, just as innocently.

Fliss looked from one to the other, and then gave it up as a bad job.

"I don't see why we couldn't have told Frankie's mum what happened," she grumbled, rubbing her shin.

"Because grown-ups just say things like 'Oh, ignore them'," said Frankie.

"Yeah, and they'd try to stop us getting our own back," I said. "This is our problem, and we'll decide what we're going to do about it."

"But we haven't decided anything yet," Rosie pointed out. We all sighed, and sat there in silence, sucking lemonade through our straws.

It wasn't like I hadn't thought about getting revenge on the M&Ms. In fact, I'd hardly thought about anything else all day. It would have been easy to ambush them in the girls' loos, and chuck wet paper towels at them, or do something ordinary, like putting a fake tarantula on Emma's chair. But that wouldn't be good enough. They'd set me up and got me into big trouble – and I was going to get my own back in style. That meant some serious thinking.

But at the moment, with our faces as long as a wet week-end, we weren't going to be able to decide on anything. It was time to get this sleepover going a bit. So I sucked some lemonade up through my straw, pointed it at Frankie and blew.

"Kenny!" Frankie spluttered, as lemonade squirted out all over her face. "You – you –! I'll get you for that!"

She sucked up some lemonade furiously, and blew. I ducked, and it hit Lyndz instead.

"Ow!" Lyndz squealed. "It's gone in my eye! It stings!"

To get her own back on Frankie, Lyndz began to suck some lemonade up her straw, too. But she sucked too hard, and began to choke. Rosie slapped her on the back, but a bit too much, and Lyndz pitched forward and got the straw stuck up her nose. The rest of us nearly died laughing.

I bet you can guess what happened next, can't you?

"Now – hic – I've got hiccups!" Lyndz groaned, when she was finally able to speak. "Frankie – hic – help me!"

"Try drinking from the other side of your glass," Fliss suggested. "That's supposed to work."

Lyndz picked up her glass, and turned it round.

"Like – hic – this, you mean?"

"No, dummy!" I said. "You hold the glass normally, but you try to drink from the opposite side."

Lyndz bent forward and tried to take a sip, but she tipped the glass up too much, and ended up pouring lemonade all down her T-shirt. The rest of us cried with laughter.

"This is really stupid, Fliss!" Lyndz yelled, creasing up herself. "It'll never work!"

"It already has!" said Fliss smugly.

"Come on," I said, grabbing Frankie's arm. "Let's play one of our International Gladiators' games on the lawn!"

Nobody mentioned the M&Ms and what had happened again for a long while after that. We had a few rounds of International Gladiators, then it started to rain so we went inside and played tapes and had a disco. Frankie's mum let us make popcorn after all, and we scoffed two huge bowls of it while we watched a video.

We were all tucked up in bed before we got talking about getting revenge on the M&Ms again. Frankie was in her own bed, and me and Lyndz were in the bunks, me on top and Lyndz at the bottom. Fliss was in the camp bed, and Rosie was in her sleeping bag on the floor. Mrs Thomas said goodnight and turned the light off, then we waited a few minutes and switched our torches on.

"Are we eating first?" Lyndz asked, opening her sleepover bag, and pulling out a packet of chocolate digestives. "I'm starving."

"No, wait a minute," I said. "I've been thinking!"

"You probably want to lie down and have a rest then," said Frankie.

"Ha, ha. No, I've been thinking about the M&Ms."

"I've had an idea about that," said Rosie. "Why don't we do the same to them when it's their turn to use the computer?"

"No, we've got to do something different," Frankie insisted. "We don't want to copy them."

"We could hide Emma's violin," Lyndz suggested. "Then we won't have to listen to her playing it in Assembly."

"I think we ought to get them into trouble with Mrs Weaver somehow," said Fliss. "After all, that's what they did to Kenny."

"What do you think, Kenny?" Frankie looked at me.

"I don't think we should do anything," I said.

The others looked shocked.

"What?" said Frankie. "Nothing at all?"

"No, I mean I don't think we should do anything just yet." I grinned at the others. "I think we should wait. Until the sleepover at the museum next week."

Everyone looked puzzled.

"Why?" asked Lyndz.

I shrugged. "Think about it. There's lots of spooky things in the museum, loads of places to hide and we'll be there all night. We're sure to be able to think of some way of getting our own back on the M&Ms while we're there. And best of all–!"

"What?" said the others.

"Well, we're excellent at sleepovers!" I pointed out. "We've been to loads. The M&Ms haven't."

"So we'll be one up on them before we start," said Frankie.

"We sure will!" I looked round at everyone, and we were all smiling. "The M&Ms are in for the biggest shock of their whole lives!"

# CHAPTER FOUR

So we didn't do anything. We just waited. It nearly killed us, but we stuck it out. Of course, the M&Ms thought it was a big joke. They were so smug, it was unbearable. Every time we went anywhere near them, they kept making chicken noises and flapping their arms. It was really difficult not to have a go at them, I can tell you. Frankie and Fliss actually had to sit on me to stop me leaping on Emma Hughes when they were winding us up in the playground one afternoon.

But as the day of the museum sleepover got nearer, a funny thing happened. The

M&Ms started to look nervous. I don't think they'd guessed we were going to get our own back on the trip; they were just worried that we hadn't done anything to them so far, and they were beginning to wonder what we were planning. They kept on staring suspiciously at us, and I'd noticed that every time they had to open their lockers, they did it really carefully, as if they expected something nasty to fall out.

Did they really think they were gonna get away with something as ordinary as that? No chance. I had something much more special in mind for them. The trouble was, I wasn't quite sure what, yet. Not until we got to the museum.

At last the Great Day arrived.

"I'm really looking forward to this," I said to Frankie, as we waited for the coach to turn up. We were sitting on our table in the classroom. We aren't usually allowed to do that, of course, but I don't think Mrs Weaver would have noticed if we'd stood up on the tables and had a disco, because she was rushing round like she had ants in her pants, trying to organise everything.

Everyone was so excited, the noise was deafening. We all had our sleeping bags, torches, pyjamas and slippers, and big bags of food for tonight. There were some parents coming with us, as well as Mrs Weaver, so the classroom was packed.

"Oh, this is going to be ace," said Rosie happily. "I can't wait to see the Egyptian mummies!"

Fliss looked a bit sick again.

"As long as we don't have to sleep in the same room as them," she said firmly.

"We'll see about that," I said under my breath to Frankie, who grinned and winked at me.

"I wonder who'll be our group leader?" Lyndz said. "I hope we don't get Mrs Weaver. She's got eyes in the back of her head."

"Yeah, we don't want anyone too smart, do we?" I lowered my voice. "Not if we're going after the M&Ms."

"Maybe we'll get one of the parents," said

Fliss.

"Yeah, isn't Alana Banana's mum coming?" said Frankie. "Alana's pretty dozy, so maybe her mum is, too."

We all looked over at Alana Banana. Banana isn't really her surname. It's Palmer. Alana Banana's pretty harmless, but she does hang around with the M&Ms sometimes, which makes her sort of our enemy. Except that she's too clueless to bother us much.

"Mrs Banana isn't here yet, is she?" said Lyndz, looking round.

"No, and anyway, she'll probably be looking after Alana's group," Frankie pointed out.

Just then we realised that Mrs Weaver was trying to get everybody's attention by yelling "QUIET!" and waving her clipboard around like a flag. We all shut up and looked at her.

"Right, the coach will be here in about ten minutes," Mrs Weaver said briskly. "Before we go, I'll tell you the name of the adult who's in charge of your group." She looked over at the M&Ms. "Emma Hughes' group, you'll be with me."

Frankie glanced at me, and pulled a face. At least we weren't in Mrs Weaver's group – that would have been a mega disaster – but the M&Ms were. That might make our plans for revenge a little bit tricky. It depended who our group leader was.

"Francesca Thomas's group." Mrs Weaver looked over at us. "You'll be with Miss Hill."

We all cheered. If I tell you that Miss Hill's a student teacher, you'll know why. You can get away with murder with a student teacher. Miss Hill, who was standing next to Mrs Weaver, turned bright pink. She probably thought we were cheering because we liked her so much. We did like her. But we liked her even more because she wasn't as clued up as Mrs W.

"Excellent!" I whispered in Frankie's ear. "Now we're all set!"

"Alana Palmer's group," Mrs Weaver went on. "You'll be with Alana's mum – where is your mum, by the way, Alana?"

Alana Banana frowned.

"She can't come, Miss."

Mrs Weaver nearly dropped down dead with shock.

"What do you mean, she can't come? It was all arranged!"

"I told you this morning that she couldn't come," said Alana.

Mrs Weaver turned purple. "No, you did not tell me, Alana!"

Alana Banana looked puzzled. "Oh, didn't I? I thought I did!"

I've never heard a teacher say a rude word, but I think Mrs Weaver came pretty close.

"I'll have to go and see who I can round up," she said to Miss Hill. "We've got to have one adult for each group of five children. Just keep an eye on them, will you?"

Mrs Weaver raced out of the room faster than Linford Christie, and headed off down the corridor.

"Now don't make too much noise," said Miss Hill, but nobody could hear her because we were all chattering.

"That Alana Banana's a real nerd," said

Frankie. "It'd serve her right if Mrs Weaver left her group behind."

Mrs Weaver didn't come back for ages. We were all beginning to get a bit fed up, when we saw the coach pull into the playground.

"Here's the coach!" yelled Rosie. "Time to go!"

Everyone cheered, grabbed their bags and headed for the door.

"I think we ought to wait for Mrs Weaver," said Miss Hill timidly, but no-one listened to her. It was a good job she wasn't standing in front of the door either, or she'd probably have been trampled on. The whole class piled out of the classroom, and charged for the coach. The driver saw us coming, looked a bit nervous and shut the doors, so we had to queue up instead. Luckily the Sleepover Club managed to get to the front.

"I want to sit at the back," I said.

Fliss groaned. "I get sick on the back seat. Anyway, there's only room for four."

"Oh, we can all sit together if we squash up," said Lyndz.

"My group wants to sit at the back," said Ryan Scott, who was standing behind us, trying to push in.

Fliss giggled, but the rest of us glared at him.

"No chance," I said. Then, right at that moment, I noticed Frankie's mum coming across the playground towards us.

"Hey, Frankie," I said, elbowing her in the ribs. "What have you forgotten?"

"What?" Frankie looked puzzled.

"You must have forgotten something," I teased her. "Here's your mum."

Frankie frowned. "What's she doing here?"

"Will you please queue up properly without pushing, or I'll send you back into class!" yelled Mrs Weaver, who'd just come out into the playground. "Sort yourselves out, please. Oh, Mrs Thomas, there you are. Thank you for filling in at such short notice."

We almost dropped down dead with shock. Frankie's mum was coming with us? That was seriously bad news. Mrs Thomas is a just bit too sharp to have around when you're planning something naughty.

"Hello, girls," said Frankie's mum. "You don't have to look quite so pleased to see me."

"Don't panic," I whispered to the others, as Mrs Weaver began telling Mrs Thomas the arrangements for the trip. "At least we're not in her group."

"Oh, Frankie," said Mrs Weaver, "I thought you'd want to be in your mum's group, so I've asked Miss Hill to take over Alana's group instead. Right, I think we're just about ready to get on the coach now."

We were all so stunned, we let Ryan Scott and his group push past us to grab the back seat. The M&Ms with Mrs Weaver, and us with Frankie's mum – were we ever going to get a chance to put our plan of revenge into action?

"Come on, girls, let's get on the coach," said Mrs Thomas. "This is going to be fun. Isn't it?"

# CHAPTER FIVE

So there we were, stuck with Frankie's mum, and there wasn't anything we could do about it. We couldn't even talk amongst ourselves, because Mrs Thomas got on the coach right behind us. Luckily, she sat right at the front next to Mrs Weaver, while we scuttled off down towards the back.

"Better luck next time, girls," said Ryan Scott smugly from the back row. We ignored him, and slid into some empty seats, me next to Fliss, and Lyndz, Rosie and Frankie squashed in together.

"I can't believe my mum's coming with

us," Frankie groaned. "Why did she have to have a day off work today?"

"What are we going to do now then?" asked Fliss urgently.

"Maybe we ought to forget the whole thing," Rosie muttered.

"Rosie's right," Lyndz agreed. "This is getting more and more dodgy."

"No way!" I said. "Don't be a bunch of wimps."

The others looked at me. They weren't convinced.

"It's too risky," Frankie said at last. "The museum's going to be crawling with grown-ups. And one of them will be my mum."

"So?" I shrugged. "There are always grown-ups around when we have our sleepovers. Have we ever let that stop us doing exactly what we want?"

"Kenny's right," said Fliss. "We can't give up now."

If I hadn't already been sitting down, I think I would have fallen down with shock. Fliss was the last person I would've expected to back me up.

"Thanks, Fliss!" I said, giving her a friendly punch on the arm.

"Ow!" Fliss clutched her elbow. "Do you mind!"

"D'you think we can get away with it?" Lyndz asked doubtfully.

"Yeah, I think we should go for it!" I said. "Leave it to me. I'll think of something that'll completely trash the M&Ms, and fool all the grown-ups."

The others grinned.

"OK, then, Kenny," said Frankie. "But it'd better not be anything too wild, because if my mum finds out we're up to something, I'm dead."

From the moment the coach pulled up outside Armfield Museum, and we all piled out, I was on the look out for possibilities. The museum's a big place – it's in a kind of old country house with lots of rooms – and I was pretty sure that, sooner or later, I'd get a brilliant idea. I didn't know what yet, but I'd know when I did. If you see what I mean.

We all followed Mrs Weaver into the museum, where we left our bags in the cloakroom.

"Get into your groups now, please," called Mrs Weaver. "The museum's Education Officer is going to give us a guided tour."

There was a lot of pushing and shoving and giggling as everyone tried to get back into their groups. All the parents were fussing, and trying to get the kids who were with them to stand in rows and shut up. Frankie's mum didn't fuss, though. She just looked us over, said, "Everyone all right?", and then left us alone.

"Your mum's so cool, Frankie," Lyndz whispered. "For a mum, I mean."

"Yeah, but she won't be so cool if she figures out we're planning a raid on the M&Ms," Frankie whispered back. "She'll be steaming mad."

"We'll have to make sure she doesn't find out then, won't we?" I said with a wink.

The museum Education Officer, Mrs Saunders, took us on the guided tour. She made it pretty interesting by telling us loads of stories and jokes about the different things the museum had, but I wasn't really listening. That was because 1) I'd been on the guided tour about a zillion times before, and 2) I was busy keeping my eyes open for something I could use to blow the M&Ms away.

At first I didn't see anything. We went into the Costume Rooms, the Doll Gallery, the Roman Room and all the other rooms, and I was starting to get worried. Maybe I'd made a mistake thinking that the museum would be a good place to play a trick on the M&Ms!

It wasn't until we went into the last room, which was the Egyptian Room, that things really started to hot up. There were loads of glass cases round the wall with things in them like old pots, gold jewellery and big stone cats. And right in the middle, lying on a platform, were six big, painted mummy cases. One of them had glass in the top, and if you looked through it, you could see the bandaged mummy lying inside. Mrs Saunders started telling us about how the Egyptians used to make dead bodies into mummies by taking out all their insides, and using a special liquid, so the bodies didn't rot away. Fliss didn't like that one bit. She turned green, and went to hide behind Frankie's mum. I knew all about mummies, but I didn't mind hearing it again, because it was so gruesome. So it took me a little while to suss out that Fliss wasn't the only one who was looking a bit icky. I nudged Frankie.

"Look at the M&Ms," I whispered in her ear.

Emma and Emily were both looking a bit sick. Not only that, they both looked scared, and they were standing really close to Mrs Weaver. They were both staring at the mummy cases as if they expected a mummy to jump out there and then, and grab them, like something in a horror film.

"They look like they're wetting themselves," Frankie whispered back.

"They are," I said. "And I think I've just sussed out our plan of revenge."

"What?" asked Rosie eagerly.

I opened my mouth to tell them, saw Frankie's mum looking at us and decided to wait till later. We were taken off to the museum café to have some juice and biscuits, and Frankie's mum left us on our own, while she went to talk to Mrs Saunders. That gave us a chance to get stuck into our plans.

"I've had this radical idea," I said, after I'd looked over my shoulder to check that the M&Ms (and Mrs Weaver) were nowhere around. "Did you see how freaked out the Gruesome Twosome were by the mummies?"

Fliss shook her head. "I didn't notice."

"That's because you were hiding behind Frankie's mum," said Lyndz.

"Well, anyway, they were dead scared," I went on. "And I reckon that's how we can get our own back on them."

"How?" said the others together.

I hadn't really sussed out the details yet, but I'd had one idea which I thought was excellent.

"Well," I said, "I thought I could hide inside one of the mummy cases and – "

I didn't get a chance to say any more, because the others nearly had a fit.

"Get serious, Kenny!" said Frankie. "Those mummy cases are worth loads of money! If you damage one of them – "

"We'll be paying for it out of our pocket money for the next zillion years," Lyndz finished off.

Fliss was almost fainting with fear.

"And what if you got stuck inside?" she gasped.

"Yeah, you'd probably suffocate," Rosie pointed out anxiously.

"Oh, all right!" I said crossly. I guess I hadn't really thought this thing through. "OK, stupid idea. But I still think we can use the mummies to get back at the M&Ms..."

And I was right. After we'd finished our juice and biscuits, Mrs Saunders took us to the activities room. There were paints, paper, glue and scissors on the tables, as well as loads of big cardboard boxes.

"We're going to make some masks," announced Mrs Saunders. "You can choose to make a mask of anything you've seen in the museum today, and I've got some postcards here to help you. If anyone would like to copy one of the painted faces of the Egyptian mummies, that would make rather a good mask."

And then, like a light bulb being switched on above my head, THAT was when I got my brilliant idea.

# CHAPTER SIX

I couldn't tell the others about my totally brilliant plan straightaway, because everyone was rushing round the room, grabbing cardboard boxes and glue and scissors. There was also a fight over the postcards, because almost everyone wanted to make a mummy mask, so Mrs Saunders had to go off to the museum shop to fetch some more. That all fitted in nicely with my plan.

"OK, Kenny," Frankie said, when we were all sitting round our worktable, heaped with model-making materials. "You've been grinning all over your face for the last five minutes. What's going on?"

"I've got it!" I said, lowering my voice, just in case. There was more noise going on in the room than in the monkey house at the zoo, but it was best to be on the safe side. "I've thought of something that's going to send the M&Ms off their heads!"

"What?" the others asked eagerly.

I shrugged. I was enjoying keeping them in suspense.

"Tell you later," I said. "I'm going to make my mask first."

The others looked disappointed.

"Oh, go on, Kenny, tell us!" begged Fliss.

"I bet she hasn't really thought of a plan, anyway," said Frankie.

I grinned, and stuck my tongue out at her.

"Oh, yes, I have, Francesca Thomas. But, like I said, I'll tell you later." I turned to Lyndz. I was going to need help to get my plan going, and I reckoned Lyndz would be best. "Let's work together, Lyndz."

"All right," Lyndz agreed cheerfully. "Which mask do you want to make then?"

"This one." I showed her the postcard I'd chosen. It was one of the painted mummy faces, the one which I thought was the scariest. It had a gold and blue headdress, and big, staring eyes, which were outlined in black.

"Oh, that's gross!" Fliss shuddered. "I wouldn't make one of those for a zillion pounds. I'm going to make a mask of one of the Victorian dolls in the doll gallery."

"Me and Frankie'll help you," Rosie offered.

Frankie pulled a face. "I'd rather make a mummy mask, like Kenny and Lyndz."

"OK, you can help us, then." I picked up a cardboard box, and put it over my head. It was so big, it covered my top half down to my shoulders. "I reckon this'll do, for starters."

"It suits you," Frankie said. "But maybe we ought to get on with the mask."

"Ha, ha," I said from inside the box. "I mean, we can make the mask out of this."

I lifted the box off, just as the M&Ms were walking past our table.

"Ooh, Emily!" Emma Hughes squealed,

rolling her eyes dramatically. "Look at that horrible mask Kenny's wearing!"

"No, I think that's just her face, isn't it?" said Emily with a stupid grin, right on cue, and they both started laughing like drains.

"You two are so funny," I said. "If you want a really good laugh, why don't you take a look at yourselves in a mirror?"

That wiped the grins off their faces, and the others began to giggle.

"Hey, Emma," The Queen was determined to have the last word, "what's Kenny's favourite food?"

"Oh, that's got to be Kentucky Fried Chicken," burbled The Goblin, and the two of them walked off, flapping their arms and squawking.

"I hope this plan of yours is totally brilliant, Kenny," said Frankie, clenching her fists, "Because the Gruesome Twosome are getting well out of control."

"Oh, it is," I said confidently. "Come on, let's get on with our mask."

Even with Frankie helping me and Lyndz, it

was a bit of a rush to get the mask finished. But by the time Mrs Thomas told us to start tidying up because it was time to eat, the mask was just about ready. I'd wanted Lyndz to help me because she's totally *coo*-ell at arty stuff, and she'd done all the cutting and sticking of the cardboard box, to make it into the shape of the mummy's headdress. Frankie's not bad at art either, and she'd painted the mummy's face on. It looked just like the real thing. I'm pathetic at anything like that, so I'd stuck to the easy bits, painting the blue and gold stripes on the headdress.

"Hey, that's excellent," said Rosie, when she and Fliss came over to take a look. "Can I try it on?"

I shook my head. "No, the paint's still a bit wet."

Fliss shuddered. "It looks just like the real one," she said.

"I know," I said. "If you saw it in the dark, in the middle of the night, you'd be dead scared, wouldn't you?"

Fliss nodded. "I think I'd die!"

I grinned. "I reckon that mask would scare anybody!" I looked round at the others to see if they'd picked up what I meant. But they were all staring at me blankly.

Then Frankie grinned. "You're going to use the mask to frighten the M&Ms out of their skins!" she said.

"Right first time," I agreed. I looked round at the others. "Is that a totally ace plan or what?"

"That's brilliant!" said Rosie and Lyndz together. Only Fliss looked a bit nervous.

"Kenny, I don't think that's a very good idea –" she began, but she didn't get a chance to say any more, because Mrs Weaver called for silence.

"Leave your masks on the tables to dry, and you can take them home with you tomorrow morning," she said. "Now we have to decide which groups are sleeping where tonight." Everyone started muttering and whispering in excited voices. As far as I could make out, almost every kid in the class wanted to sleep over in the Egyptian room with the mummies.

Mrs Weaver picked up her clipboard, and studied it.

"Would any group like to sleep in the Doll Gallery?" she asked hopefully.

The M&Ms's hands went up. So did Fliss's. Well, it did until Frankie grabbed her wrist, and pulled it down.

"Emma, I think your hand was up first," said Mrs Weaver. "Your group can go and get your bags, and take them to the gallery now."

Fliss glared at Frankie. "I wanted to sleep in the Doll Gallery," she moaned.

We all ignored her.

"Who'd like to sleep in the Egyptian room?" Mrs Weaver went on.

My hand flew up into the air, and so did about twenty-five others.

"Kenny, I think you were first," said Mrs Weaver. Everyone else in the class groaned loudly. "Your group can go and collect your bags."

"Go and get your things, girls," said Mrs Thomas, coming up behind us. "I'm going to the café to have a cup of tea."

We went to the cloakroom to get our stuff, and then we carried it down the corridor to the Egyptian room. We dumped them in a corner, and I pulled the door shut, so that we were finally on our own, away from all the interfering grown-ups.

"Right!" I said. "Now we can talk about Operation Gruesome Twosome!"

Fliss was looking nervously around the room.

"I'm never going to get to sleep in here!" she muttered.

"Don't worry, Fliss," said Frankie, "the mummies don't make any noise."

"No," I agreed, "except when they're moaning and wailing and trying to frighten people to death."

Fliss groaned. "Stop it, Kenny!"

"So, what's the plan, Kenny?" asked Lyndz.

I already had it all worked out.

"We wait till Frankie's mum's asleep, then

we sneak out, get the mask and take it to the doll gallery." I grinned round at the others. "Then we tap it against the window, and frighten the M&Ms out of their stupid little skins!"

Everyone started giggling.

"What about Mrs Weaver?" asked Lyndz. "She's going to be in with the M&Ms, isn't she?"

I shrugged. "I'll have the mask on, so even if she wakes up, she won't know it's me. The rest of you will have to make sure you keep out of sight."

"Won't Mrs Weaver recognise your mask?" asked Rosie.

I shook my head. "No, about half the class have made the same mask we did. Anyway, it's going to be pretty dark."

"What about Frankie's mum?" asked Fliss. "She might wake up when we sneak out."

"We'll have to risk it," I said. "The other thing is, we'll have to wait until we're sure everyone's asleep, not just Frankie's mum."

"I'll never be able to keep awake," said Fliss.

"I could set my watch alarm," offered Rosie.

"Yeah, and have Frankie's mum wake up as well?" I pointed out.

"Oh, I can wake everyone up," Lyndz said confidently. "I've got this brilliant system for getting myself up without an alarm clock. You just bang your head on your pillow six times if you want to wake up at six o'clock, and it works. It's magic!"

"Right, let's make it two o'clock then," I said. "Now we're set!"

But this is the Sleepover Club, right? And nothing's ever that simple!

# CHAPTER SEVEN

I opened my eyes, and blinked. For a minute, I couldn't remember where I was. Then, through the darkness I saw the shadows of the mummy cases all lined up on the platform. I wasn't scared, though. I mean, I have to look at Molly-the-Monster's ugly face every morning. So why should I be scared of a load of old mummies?

I didn't know how long I'd been asleep, but Lyndz hadn't woken us up yet, so it couldn't have been very long. I looked round at the others. They were all asleep, curled up in their sleeping bags. We were all lying in a row next to the platform which had the mummy cases on. Guess who was the furthest away? Yeah, go to the top of the class. Flissy Baby wasn't taking any chances, just in case one of the mummies fancied a midnight feast.

I raised myself on my elbow, and looked cautiously across the room. Frankie's mum was over the other side of the platform, and it looked like she was fast asleep, too. She'd been a bit surprised last night that we were so keen to go to bed, and that we didn't want to stay awake for ages chatting, like everyone else was doing. Still, I don't think she suspected anything was going on!

The museum was dead quiet now, though. Everyone had to be asleep, even Ryan Scott's group, who were in the Roman Room next door. They'd kept trying to frighten us after lights out by tapping on the wall. Boys. They're s-o-o-o-o pathetic.

I rolled over, and picked up my watch, and my eyes nearly popped right out of my head. Half past four!!! What had happened to Lyndz's 'brilliant' system to wake everybody up? I leaned over and shook Frankie, who was lying next to me. When she opened her eyes, I waved my watch in front of her face.

"It's half-past four!" I mouthed silently, pointing at the door.

Frankie nodded, and shook Rosie, who was next to her. Rosie woke Lyndz up, and Lyndz sat up, yawning and looking puzzled.

"It's not two o'clock, is it?" she whispered.

"No, it's half-past four!" I whispered back. "Great waking-up system, Lyndz!"

"We'd better go," Frankie said, sliding out of her sleeping bag. "It'll be getting light soon."

Lyndz rolled over, and poked Fliss. Fliss opened her eyes, took one look at the mummy cases, and let out a little scream. Lyndz lunged across and tried to stop her, but it was too late.

We all froze, waiting for Frankie's mum to sit up and ask us what was going on. But she didn't. We heard her roll over in her sleeping bag, and then there was silence.

We didn't even dare sigh with relief. Instead we just got to our feet, and tiptoed over to the door, which was so heavy, Frankie and I had to hold it open to let everyone slip silently out. When we were all safely outside in the corridor, we sighed with relief.

"Sorry," Fliss said shakily. "The mummies nearly scared me to death."

"From now on, we've got to be really quiet," I whispered. "If anyone wakes up, we're dead."

We had to get the mask first, so we tiptoed down the dimly-lit corridor to the activities room, hardly daring to breathe. We had to go past the Roman Room, where Ryan Scott's group were sleeping, and past the Art Gallery, where Alana Banana's group were with Miss Hill. Luckily, the doors were closed.

The activities room was really dark, but we didn't dare put the light on. The others waited by the door, while I groped my way round the tables, trying to find our mask. Frankie was holding the door open, so there was a bit of light from the corridor, but not much.

"Hurry up, Kenny," Fliss was moaning, "if we get caught, Mrs Weaver'll never let us go on another school trip ever again."

"Oh, great big fat hairy deal," I muttered. I was feeling my way round the tables, and knocking things over, including a pot of glue. "Oh, rats! Now I've got glue all over my hand!"

"Never mind that," said Frankie. "Just get a move on!"

I found the mask, and hurried back over to the door. "Got it!" I said triumphantly.

Fliss took one look at the mask, and stepped behind Frankie.

"Keep that thing away from me, Kenny!" she hissed, giving me a dirty look.

"It's that scary, huh?" I slipped the mask over my head. "Let's see what it looks like when it's on."

Lyndz had neatly cut out the big eyes, so that I could see through them. The others looked impressed (except Fliss, of course).

"It's brilliant!" said Frankie. "The M&Ms are going to wet themselves!"

"Serves them right!" said Rosie.

I took the mask off again, and put it under my arm.

"Come on, then. What's the quickest way to

the Doll Gallery?"

"We can take a short cut through the Costume Rooms," said Fliss.

So we tiptoed along the corridor to the Costume Rooms. We got lost a few times, because there were so many twists and turns, but eventually we made it. Frankie pushed the door open a little way, and then froze.

"What's biting you?" I began.

"SSHHH!" Frankie hissed. "There's someone in there!"

"It's a ghost!" moaned Fliss, clutching Lyndz's arm.

"Ow!" said Lyndz. "Let go, you're hurting me!"

"QUIET!" ordered Frankie, in a whisper that was louder than anyone. She let the door swing softly back into place. "Caroline Powell's group's in there, with her mum. We'll have to go a different way."

I thought for a minute. It was lucky we'd been to the museum so many times before, and knew our way around.

"We'll have to double back, and cut through

that room that's got all the statues in it. Come on."

We hurried back down the corridor, and after a few false starts, we made it to the right room. Frankie pulled the door open just a bit, and checked that none of our class were sleeping inside, then we all went in. It was a big room, with a large window in the ceiling, and a light had been left on, although it wasn't very bright. There were white stone statues of people and animals all round the room. Some were just heads, but others were really big, reaching almost to the ceiling.

"I don't like this," said Fliss nervously, as we walked through the room towards the door on the opposite side. "They're all staring at me."

"They're statues, dummy," I said. "They're not real."

"They might be," said Fliss. "They might come to life at night."

"Oh, grow up, Flissy," I said impatiently. "Anway, even if they did, what do you think they're going to do?"

"They'd probably go and find some clothes," said Rosie, with a grin. "They look pretty cold."

That made Fliss giggle. "They could definitely do with some underwear," she said, and the others started to giggle too.

"Oh, grow up and shut up!" I sighed, reaching for the door. "Everyone ready?"

Fliss was still giggling, so I gave her the evil eye until she stopped. Then we slipped out into the corridor.

"Which way do we go now?" Rosie asked.

"That way," said Frankie, pointing right.

"That way," said Fliss at exactly the same moment, pointing left.

We went right, because Frankie usually knows best. But we had to go quite a long way down the corridor before we got to the Doll Gallery.

"This is it!" I said quietly, as we stopped in front of the doors. My heart was pounding with excitement. I'd waited a long time to get my revenge on the M&Ms, and now I was going to enjoy it. "I'm going to take a look inside, and find out where the M&Ms are."

"Be careful," said Frankie.

I laid the mask carefully on the floor, and put my face to the glass at the top of the door. I could just about see in. The room was quite dark, but someone had left their torch on, so I got a pretty good view. The dolls were in glass cases all around the walls, and there were six sleeping bags dotted in different places around the room. The M&Ms were in the perfect place, not far from the door where I was looking in. Best of all, Mrs Weaver was right over the other side of the room.

"Ace!" I whispered to the others. "The M&Ms are right here, and Mrs Weaver's miles away!"

"I want to see!" said Fliss.

"Me too," said Rosie. "I want to watch the M&Ms faces when they see Kenny in the mask!"

I shook my head. "No way," I said. "They'll see you for sure."

"Hang on a minute," said Frankie. "We could

go round the side, and look through the curtains."

There was a long row of windows at the side of the gallery, where the curtains had been drawn, but they didn't quite meet.

"Go on, then," I hissed. "But make sure you don't get spotted."

It was all right for me, I had the mask to hide behind, but I didn't want the others to get caught.

I waited till the others were in position at the side windows, and Frankie gave me a thumbs-up. Then I picked up the mask, and slid it over my head. I got it into position so that I could see through the cut-out eyes, and then I peered through the window at the top of the door. The M&Ms were only a few yards away. In fact, they were so close that I could hear Emma Hughes snoring.

I took a deep breath, and tapped on the glass!

# CHAPTER EIGHT

At first, neither of the M&Ms woke up. So I tapped a little bit louder. I was a bit worried I might wake up someone else in the room first, but no-one stirred.

Then Emma Hughes stopped snoring, and started to move about a bit inside her sleeping bag. I tapped again.

Emma opened her eyes, and looked straight at me. I mean, she looked straight at the mummy mask peering in at her through the glass.

Emma's mouth fell open. She looked as if she was trying to scream, but she was so terrified, she couldn't make a sound. I wanted to burst out laughing, but of course I couldn't.

I saw Emma grab Emily's arm. Emily woke up, looked at me and let out a roar that must've woken everyone else in the museum up.

"AAGGGH! IT'S THE MUMMY!!!"

Oh, it was BRILLIANT! They both looked totally scared out of their skins, and Emma Hughes started crying. I wanted to stay and watch them a bit longer, but Mrs Weaver had woken up now, and was putting her dressing gown on. Time to leg it, if we knew what was good for us. I ducked down out of sight, just as Frankie and the others did the same at the other windows.

"Did you see their faces!" Fliss whispered, red-faced from trying not to giggle.

"That's the best trick we've ever done!" said Lyndz.

"And now we've got to get out of here," I said urgently. "Mrs Weaver's awake."

We were just about to make a run for it,

when we heard Mrs Weaver talking inside the room.

"Whatever's the matter, Emma?" we heard her say.

"It was the mummy, Miss!" Emily gasped. Emma was weeping too much to say anything. "It's alive! It was looking through the window at us!"

We all clutched at each other, and bit hard on our lips to stop ourselves laughing.

"Oh really?" Mrs Weaver said in a grim voice. "We'll see!"

And then we heard her walk over to the door. Boy, did we stop laughing straightaway.

"Leg it!" I hissed at the others.

We ran. We skidded off down the corridor at a hundred miles an hour. Luckily we made it round the corner before Mrs Weaver opened the door.

"Who's there?" we heard her say sharply. I prayed that she'd go back in, shut the door and tell the M&Ms that they'd dreamt it. But she didn't. Next thing was, we heard her coming down the corridor after us!

"We've got to get back to our sleeping bags!" Frankie said urgently. "Quick!" She opened the door of one of the galleries. "In here!"

"This isn't the room with the statues that we came through before," I said.

"Never mind, we'll find our way back somehow." Frankie pushed me inside, and the others followed.

The room was in complete darkness.

"Why didn't we bring our torches!" said Rosie. "Where are we?"

"Sssh!" said Lyndz. "I can hear Mrs Weaver going past!"

We all held our breath. Mrs Weaver hurried past the room we were in, and turned the corner.

"I bet she's going to check up on all the other groups," said Frankie. "We've got to get back to the Egyptian Room before she does!"

"It'd help if we could see where we were," I said. I stretched out a hand in the darkness – and it touched something furry. I managed not to scream, but I wasn't far off.

"What is it, Kenny?" asked Rosie, who'd heard me give a little yelp.

"I touched something furry!" I gasped.

"I'm scared!" Fliss moaned. "What is it?"

"If I could see it, I'd tell you!" I snapped. I stretched out my hand again, and felt the furry thing. It was pretty gross feeling something like that in the dark, a bit like that game we play at sleepovers sometimes – you know the one, where someone's blindfolded and you give them really gruesome objects, and they have to guess what they are. I gave Fliss some cold spaghetti once, and told her it was worms. She nearly passed out.

Anyway, I forced myself to keep feeling the furry thing, and then I guessed what it was.

"It's a stuffed animal!" I said, relieved. "I think we're in the animals gallery."

"Ugh! Gross!" said Fliss. "Let's get out of here."

"I think there's a door on the other side," said Frankie. "Hold hands so we can keep together, and I'll see if I can find it."

We inched our way through the darkness,

with Frankie at the front.

"Here's the door," said Frankie, sounding mightily relieved. She pulled it open a little way, and checked the coast was clear. Next second, we were out in the dim light of another corridor.

"Are we lost?" asked Lyndz anxiously.

I tried to think. I knew the museum really well, but right now my brain just wouldn't work.

"I think we go this way," I said, pointing down the corridor. And that was when we heard the noise again. Footsteps, coming towards us. Fliss squealed with fright, and the footsteps started to run.

"Quick, in here!" Frankie opened the door of the nearest room, and bundled us all inside. Fliss's knees were shaking so much, Rosie had to drag her in after the rest of us. This time the room was lit, and we could see it was full of broken old pots, that someone had put back together, like jigsaw puzzles.

"That way!" I hissed frantically, pointing to a door on the other side of the room. We raced over to it on tiptoe. As Frankie pulled it open, we heard the door we'd just come in at start to open!

This time Fliss was too terrified even to make a sound, and the rest of us weren't far behind. We scuttled through the door, and Frankie pulled it shut. There was another gallery opposite us, and I reached for the door handle. I didn't know which room it was, and I didn't care. I just flung the door open.

"Not in there!" gasped Rosie, leaping forward and pulling it shut. Before it closed, I saw why. It was the Science Room, and there were kids from our class in sleeping bags all over the floor.

"What's going on?" we heard someone say sleepily, as Rosie shut the door, and then we heard the sound of torches being switched on.

"Everyone in the museum's going to be awake at this rate!" I said through my teeth. "Frankie, do something!"

Frankie looked as frantic as I was feeling, but she bravely set off down the corridor and we all followed. Behind us we heard the sounds of lights being switched on, and people talking.

"Even if we do make it back to our room, Frankie's mum's bound to be awake," Rosie groaned.

"Maybe not," Lyndz said hopefully. "The Egyptian room's right over the other side of the building."

Frankie stopped outside yet another door, labelled "Flower Paintings".

"If we go through here, I think there's a short cut back to the mummies," she said. She didn't sound too sure, but nobody was about to argue. We all bundled into the room, and closed the door behind us.

It was a long room, with old paintings of flowers in big vases along the walls. There were loads of windows, and it was starting to get a bit lighter outside, so at least we could see where we were going now. The only problem was, there were six doors all along the room.

"Which door is it?" asked Fliss through

chattering teeth.

Frankie looked at me, and I looked at Frankie. This was one of the rooms that Mrs Saunders hadn't taken us into on this visit, so we had to try and remember from one of our other trips.

"The one at the end of the room!" we both said together.

"It comes out into another gallery with paintings in it, and that's right opposite the Egyptian room," Frankie added.

The others all sighed with relief. We raced down the long room towards the very last door, and skidded to a halt. But as we got nearer, we could see that there was a sign on the door.

THIS GALLERY IS CLOSED
FOR RE-DECORATION

We all groaned. Rosie reached out, and rattled the handle, but the door was locked.

"What now?" squeaked Fliss. "There must be another way back!"

"We'll have to try one of the other doors," Frankie panted. I'd never seen her look so wound up – she's usually dead cool. Mind you, I wasn't exactly having a laugh myself. I knew just how ballistic Mrs Weaver would go if she caught us!

Frankie yanked open the door nearest to us, and we dived through into another gallery. It was full of those metal suits of armour, all standing up in long rows. Fliss clutched at my hand.

"I hate these," she muttered. "I always think there's really people inside them."

Fliss is a bit of a wimp, but this time I knew what she meant. We were halfway along the corridor, when Fliss, who was still clutching my hand, dug her nails in. Hard.

"Ow!" I tried to pull away from her, but Fliss was hanging onto me like a limpet. "What's biting you?"

"That – that suit of armour," Fliss moaned. "It – it MOVED!"

"Oh, don't be so pathetic!" I snapped, but I couldn't help looking hard at the suit of armour Fliss was pointing at. So did the others. And we all shuffled forward a bit, so that we were huddled close together.

"It did!" Fliss was practically hysterical. "He lifted his hand up! I saw it!"

"Fliss, it's a suit of armour!" said Frankie. "There's no-one inside it. Look."

She reached out, and touched the metal hand. It broke away from the metal arm, and fell to the polished floor with a resounding CRASH that must have woken everybody up for five miles around.

That put the king in the cake. We ran for it. We hurtled out the other side of the gallery, and into the corridor, gasping for breath. Then we saw the sign on the door opposite.

THE EGYPTIAN ROOM

"We've made it!" I gasped. "Let's hope your mum's still asleep, Frankie."

"And that Mrs Weaver's not waiting for us behind the door," said Rosie.

We pushed open the door, hardly daring to breathe. But, unbelievably, everything was exactly the same as we'd left it. And Frankie's mum was still fast asleep in her sleeping bag on the other side of the room.

"I don't believe it!" muttered Fliss. "We did it!"

Then we heard footsteps coming down the corridor. Mrs Weaver was obviously still on the warpath.

"Move!" I hissed.

We all dived into our sleeping-bags. Two seconds later, the door opened!

# CHAPTER NINE

We all shut our eyes at exactly the same moment that Mrs Weaver looked round the door. She shone her torch into the room, and then we all pretended to wake up.

"Sorry to disturb you, girls," said Mrs Weaver. "But someone's been running around the museum playing tricks."

"Oh, really, Miss?" said Frankie, doing a great imitation of a yawn.

"Is everything all right, Mrs Weaver?" Frankie's mum had got out of her sleeping bag, and come across the room. "Has something happened?"

"Someone's been frightening the girls in my group with a mummy mask," said Mrs Weaver grimly. "I almost caught them, but then I got lost around the galleries."

I glanced at Frankie. So Mrs Weaver had got lost too. That must've been why we made it back before her. Lucky or what?

"Well, I don't think it was any of us," said Frankie's mum, looking round. "We're all here."

"So I see," said Mrs Weaver, 'I think I'll go and check on Ryan Scott's group.' And she closed the door.

"Come on, girls, let's get back to sleep," said Frankie's mum, "or you'll be dead tired in the morning."

We all snuggled down into our sleeping bags. But as soon as Mrs Thomas had gone back over to the other side of the room, we all started laughing and talking. We were just too hyped up to go to sleep right away.

"I can't believe we got back here before Mrs Weaver," whispered Fliss. "We nearly didn't make it!"

"Thank goodness she got lost as well," said Rosie, "or we'd have been nicked!"

"It was worth it though," said Lyndz. "I just wish I had a photo of Emma's face when she saw Kenny in that mask!"

We all started shaking with laughter. The more we tried to stop, the more we laughed. We had to stuff corners of our sleeping-bags in our mouths to stop ourselves from making too much noise.

"We trashed the M&Ms good and proper," I said at last, when we'd finally stopped laughing. "I bet they know it was us, too."

"Do you think so?" said Fliss, looking scared. "What if they tell Mrs Weaver?"

"So what if they do?" said Frankie. "They've got no proof."

"They might have recognised Kenny's mask," said Rosie.

"My mask!" I said suddenly.

"Girls, will you please be quiet and get some sleep?" said Mrs Thomas from across the room.

"What about your mask, Kenny?"

whispered Lyndz.

"I've lost it!" I whispered back. "I put it down somewhere when we were trying to make it back here, and I can't remember where!"

"We've got to get it back!" said Frankie urgently. "If Mrs Weaver finds it—"

"She'll know it was us who played the trick," finished Rosie.

"Where did you leave it, Kenny?" asked Lyndz.

I thought hard.

"I think I put it down on the floor when I was trying to work out what that furry thing was," I said at last. "D'you think I should go and try to get it back now?"

"NO!" said the others all together.

"Girls," said Mrs Thomas, and she was starting to sound pretty annoyed, "will you please go to sleep now."

"We'll look for it first thing tomorrow morning," Frankie whispered, and I nodded.

I wasn't really that worried. After all, somebody else could have borrowed my mask to play a trick on the M&Ms. But I didn't want Mrs Weaver getting suspicious. I wasn't her flavour of the month as it was. I didn't want to get into any more doom.

I yawned and closed my eyes. A picture of Emma and Emily's horrified faces as they looked at the mummy looking in at them came into my mind, and I started giggling into my pillow.

I was still smiling when I fell asleep.

"Kenny?"

Someone was shaking me awake. I didn't want to open my eyes, but whoever it was kept on shaking me, so I had to.

It was Rosie.

"It's ten-to-eight, and we're having breakfast in ten minutes," she said. "I think we should go and look for the mask."

"OK." I rolled out of my sleeping bag, and reached for my jeans. The others were starting to wake up too, except for Frankie, who was snoring. I gave her a kick.

"Wakey, wakey, Francesca."

"Where's my mum?"

"I think she's gone to the loo," said Rosie. "Me and Kenny are going to look for the mask."

We left the others climbing sleepily into their clothes, and headed off down the corridor.

"Let's try the stuffed animals room first," I said. "I'm pretty sure that's where I left it."

It was a lot easier to find our way around the museum in daylight. We went into the animal gallery, and looked round.

"This is gross!" said Rosie, staring at a stuffed peacock. "Why would anyone want to stuff an animal?"

"D'you want to know how they do it?" I said. "First they —"

Rosie gave me a shove. "Not before breakfast, thanks. Why are you such a weirdo, Kenny?"

"I'm just so good at it." I grinned, and took a look round the room. Most of the animals were inside glass cases, but some were just standing around on little platforms.

"I think that fox might have been the furry thing I was touching," I said, pointing across the room.

We went over to it.

"It looks a bit moth-eaten," said Rosie. "Are you sure this was where you left the mask?"

I closed my eyes, and thought hard.

"Yep," I said at last. "I remember I had the mask in one hand, and I touched the fox with the other. I didn't know what it was, so I put the mask down, so I could use both hands."

Rosie looked at me. "Well, where is it then?"

We searched all round where the fox was standing, and then all round the rest of the room, but the mask was nowhere to be seen.

"You must've left it somewhere else," Rosie said at last.

"I didn't." I knew I hadn't. I remembered putting the mask down right next to the stuffed fox. So where had it got to?

"Have you lost something, girls?"

The voice behind us made us jump a mile. We turned round. Frankie's mum was there, carrying a towel and a toothbrush.

"No, Mrs Thomas," I said innocently. "We had a bit of time before breakfast, so we came to look at the animals."

Frankie's mum glanced at her watch.

"Well, it's eight o'clock now, so we'd better go down to the café."

"What are we going to do about the mask?" Rosie whispered in my ear.

I shrugged. "Not a lot. Maybe an early-morning cleaner's chucked it in the bin or something."

We met up with the others in the café. They were already getting stuck into bowls of Coco-Pops and plates of toast.

"Did you find the mask?" was the first question Lyndz asked us.

Rosie and I shook our heads.

"It's gone," I said, "don't ask me where."

"Maybe Mrs Weaver found it," said Fliss, looking terrified.

We all stared hard at Mrs Weaver, who'd just walked in. She looked all right. Meaning, she didn't have steam coming out of her ears.

"Good morning, children," she said, with a smile.

"Looks like we're in the clear," I said to the others. Then we all started to giggle. Behind Mrs Weaver were the M&Ms. They both had black circles under their eyes, and they looked as if they hadn't had any sleep all night.

"Bad night, Emma?" I said, with a huge grin.

"Yeah, we heard about that mummy coming after you," said Frankie. "Funny, we were in the same room with it, and it didn't come after us."

"We didn't even hear it get up and go out," added Rosie, with a totally innocent look on her face."We were all fast asleep."

The M&Ms looked fit to bust, they were so furious. And that just cracked us up even more.

"We know it was you!" spluttered Emma Hughes. "You're totally pathetic!"

"And we're going to tell Mrs Weaver!" growled Emily Berryman.

"Go on then," I challenged them coolly. "You've got no proof."

The M&Ms opened and shut their mouths a few times like a couple of angry goldfish, but they knew I was right. Mrs Weaver wouldn't give them the time of day, unless they could prove for certain that it was us who'd played that trick on them.

"Hey, Emma!" Ryan Scott and his mate Danny McCloud walked into the café with their hands held out in front of them like a couple of zombies. "We've risen from the dead, and we're coming to get you!"

We all fell about. The Queen and the Goblin were going to be the joke of the whole school for the next few weeks, and didn't they deserve it. They both turned bright red, and stalked off.

"Result!" I said, holding up my hand to Frankie for a high five. Then I did the same to all the others. What a radical sleepover that had been. I'd never thought my idea would work out so brilliantly.

"More toast, anyone?" said a voice from behind us. It was Frankie's mum. That shut us all up.

"You've obviously had a good time, then," Mrs Thomas remarked after she'd handed round the toast.

"Yes, we have," we all chorused politely. She just didn't know how good.

Mrs Thomas looked pleased.

"Good. Well, when you've finished eating, go and pack your stuff away, and collect your masks. The coach is coming at nine to pick us up."

"I wish I knew where my mask had gone," I moaned to Frankie as we packed our sleeping bags away after breakfast. "I wanted to keep it as a souvenir of the night we crushed the M&Ms."

"What were you going to do, frame it and stick it on your bedroom wall?" Rosie asked.

"Something like that." I grinned evilly. "I was thinking about trying the same trick on Molly Monster-Features."

Just then Fliss and Lyndz, who'd gone to collect Fliss's mask, came in, carrying a black bin-liner. Frankie's mum was behind them.

"The coach is here, girls," she said. "Kenny,

have you collected your mask?"

That threw me. I stared at Frankie's mum, and for a second, I couldn't think of anything to say.

It was Fliss who saved the day.

"I've got the masks here, Mrs Thomas," she said, waving the black bin liner.

"Right, let's go then." Frankie's mum picked up her bags, and went out, while the rest of us sagged with relief.

"Nice one, Flissy," I said gratefully. "Thanks."

Fliss turned pink. "I'm not as stupid as I look," she said.

"No, of course not," I agreed. "Nobody could be that stupid."

We all cracked up at that, even Fliss. We picked up our bags, and I took one last look around the room.

"I wish I hadn't lost that mask," I muttered. "I don't suppose I'll ever see it again now."

Guess what? I was wrong!

# CHAPTER TEN – GOODBYE

So now I've told you almost everything that happened at the Great Museum Sleepover. Almost. But not quite.

We decided that we'd all go round to Frankie's on Saturday afternoon, so that we could talk over what had happened. Oh, and to have a good laugh at the M&Ms, of course.

It was a sunny day, so Frankie's dad had put their sun lounger out on the patio. It was one of those swinging ones, and we all piled onto it, even though it was a bit small for the five of us. It's really old as well, so it creaked every time we swung it backwards and forwards.

"I can't wait till Monday," said Fliss.

"Everyone in the whole school's going to know what happened to the M&Ms."

"And if they don't, we'll soon tell them," I said, swinging the sun lounger to and fro a little bit faster. Rosie, who was squashed in the middle and had hardly any seat at all, flew off as the seat swung back, and landed on the patio on her bottom.

"Ow!" she complained, while the rest of us howled with laughter. "Can't somebody else sit in the middle?"

We all squashed up, so that Rosie could get in on the end. Now Fliss was in the middle. I raised my eyebrows at Frankie. "How long to knock Fliss off the seat, and onto the patio?"

"Six seconds," said Frankie.

"What?" asked Fliss.

"Nothing," I said. "I don't reckon we'll get any bother from the M&Ms now for a while, do you?"

"They'll want to get their own back sometime," Lyndz said. "I've never seen Emma Hughes that mad."

"We'll be ready for them," I said, swinging the seat back as hard as I could. Fliss gave a squeal, and slid off onto the patio with a thump.

"Five seconds," said Frankie, looking at her watch. "Good one."

"Very funny," sniffed Fliss, climbing to her feet.

"What are we going to do this afternoon then?" asked Lyndz.

"Let's just sit around and talk," suggested Frankie. "I'll make us some Coca-Cola floats."

"Cool!" I said. "And I'll show you my impression of Emma Hughes' face when she saw the mummy. I've been practising it since yesterday."

I pulled open my mouth and popped out my eyes as far as they would go. The others howled.

"And this is Emily Berryman." I stopped, and put on a really deep, gruff voice. "HELP! THE MUMMY! IT'S ALIVE!!!"

I didn't get to finish my impression of Emily, because Frankie's mum came into the garden out of their garage. She was wearing old clothes and rubber gloves, and she had a black bin-liner in her hand.

"Frankie, if you girls want anything to eat, you'll have to get it yourself," Mrs Thomas said. "I'm going to make a start on cleaning out the garage."

She didn't look too happy about it, and I wasn't surprised. Frankie's family are like squirrels. They keep everything. The garage has so many boxes and bags in it that they have to park their car on the drive.

"Oh, by the way," said Mrs Thomas, "I thought you might like this."

She opened the bin-liner, and pulled out a cardboard mask. A mummy mask. My mask.

"I think it's yours, isn't it, Kenny?"

I was too gobsmacked to say anything, and so were the others. I just nodded.

"I found it in the stuffed animals gallery this morning," Frankie's mum went on. "Funny. I can't think how it got there!"

This time it was us who looked like goldfish. We opened our mouths, couldn't think of anything to say, and shut them again. Frankie's mum put the mask back in the bin-liner, and gave it to me. I knew then that she knew. Mrs Thomas knew that it was *us* who'd played that trick the night before.

The question was, what was she going to do about it?

"Well, I think I'd better get on with clearing the garage," said Frankie's mum. "Of course, I'd get on a lot quicker if you girls gave me a hand!"

"We'd love to," we all said together.

"It's a bit of a dirty job, and it's going to take a while," Mrs Thomas pointed out. "Sure you don't mind?"

"Oh, we don't mind," I said. "Not one bit."

Frankie's mum went back into the garage, and we all looked at each other.

"She knows!" babbled Fliss nervously.

"And she's let us off," Rosie added.

"Not quite," said Frankie. "You haven't seen our garage."

"Your mum knew the M&Ms played that trick on Kenny," said Lyndz. "That must be why she didn't give us away."

"Your mum's really cool, Frankie," I said.

"Yeah, but we'd better not push it," Frankie warned us, sliding off the sun lounger. "Come on, let's get started."

So that was what I mean when I said we'd sort of got away with it. Although after an afternoon clearing out Frankie's garage, I think I'd rather have been grounded for a week. It was cool of Mrs Thomas not to give us away though. Mrs Weaver would have chewed us to bits if she'd found out.

That's it. End of story. I didn't do so badly, did I? I was just as good as Frankie.

Look, there are the others over there by the playground gate. Come over, and say hello. Oh, and here come the M&Ms, with their faces down to their knees. I'm really going to enjoy this. I've been looking through all my joke books, and finding loads of jokes about mummies, so that I can annoy the Gruesome Twosome all day.

I'll catch up with you again really soon.

By-e-e-e-e!

# Order Form

To order direct from the publishers, just make a list of the titles you want and fill in the form below:

Name

..................................................................................

Address

..................................................................................

..................................................................................

..................................................................................

Send to: Dept 6, HarperCollins Publishers Ltd, Westerhill Road, Bishopbriggs, Glasgow G64 2QT.

Please enclose a cheque or postal order to the value of the cover price, plus:

UK & BFPO: Add £1.00 for the first book, and 25p per copy for each additional book ordered.

Overseas and Eire: Add £2.95 service charge. Books will be sent by surface mail but quotes for airmail despatch will be given on request.

A 24-hour telephone ordering service is available to holders of Visa, MasterCard, Amex or Switch cards on 0141- 772 2281.

Collins

An *Imprint* of HarperCollins*Publishers*